HELPING HANDS

HELPING HANDS

KEN SAIK

HELPING HANDS

iUniverse books may be ordered through booksellers or by contacting:

iUniverse
1663 Liberty Drive
Bloomington, IN 47403
www.iuniverse.com
1-800-Authors (1-800-288-4677)

ISBN: 978-1-5320-3873-0 (sc)
ISBN: 978-1-5320-3875-4 (hc)
ISBN: 978-1-5320-3874-7 (e)

Library of Congress Control Number: 2018902821

Print information available on the last page.

iUniverse rev. date: 06/01/2018

CONTENTS

LIFE'S CHANGED

As they eat lunch, Jill asks about her children's plans. She thinks they might go for a walk to the park like they used to do. After her lengthy hospital stay, she looks forward to spending some time with them.

Sarah surprises Jill by telling her that she has a part-time job at a convenience store. "Only twenty minutes by bike," she says proudly. "But I'll be home for supper."

Matt informs Jill of a fun soccer game that he and some neighborhood boys will be playing in the schoolyard. He adds that he bikes there with his friend, Bennett.

"It's a way Ben exercises Buster, his German shepherd."

Matt too promises to return before supper.

In too short a time, they finish lunch, give Jill a quick hug, and disappear into their own lives. Jill drops into her chair, haunted by the awareness that she's alone again, alone like she was in the hospital. She toys with the possibilities of how she might once again be part of her children's lives.

Focusing on the dirty lunch dishes on the counter, she gets up, grateful she has something to do. To hide her disappointment, she searches the cupboards and the fridge and writes out a grocery list. Then she realizes she has no car. *I'll have to wait until Friday evening. Amber will drive me.*

Amber, her eldest daughter, works as a flag person to earn money to go to university.

Call a physiotherapist.

Jill takes out her purse and finds the list the doctor gave her. A shadow descends on her plans. *No car. How will I follow up on my exercise program?*

Jill plops onto the kitchen chair again; her head sinks into her propped-up hands. She delays choosing a therapist. *Maybe Julie will drive me.*

Julie, her niece, won't be back from her holidays for at least another week. Thwarted, she goes down to the fitness center on the main floor of their condo. Stepping onto the treadmill, she sets a pace a third of what it used to be before her accident. As she walks, she laments. *So much has changed.* She misses planning events with her children the most. Jill worries that she might not be able to reclaim her life from a couple of months ago.

It's like trying to catch a piece of paper grabbed by the wind. They all have different lives now, lives without me, like babies pushed out of a nest, flying everywhere, anytime. She brushes a tear away. *But I didn't push them out.*

The knowledge that she has missed a valuable part of her children's lives clings to Jill like a cool, damp fog. She steps off the treadmill to catch her breath. A shiver vibrates through her.

It's like I've been robbed.

She returns to her apartment. To prevent slipping into the past, she plans supper. Assuming it will be at six o'clock like it used to be, she opens the fridge door. Leftover fruit salad, meatloaf, and potatoes tell her what the supper menu will be. Ingredients for a vegetable salad are absent. Half a homemade pizza is wrapped up on a dinner plate. *Joseph's work. Probably Amber's supper tonight.*

Healthy food choices were never a priority for her ex-husband. The moment Joseph heard Jill would be coming home, he left.

Not a problem. Jill determines to reverse Joseph's menu choices.

Amber arrives home from work after nine. Jill's face glows in response to her daughter's enthusiastic welcome. In preparation for her meal, Amber places the leftover pizza in the microwave.

"No salad?" asks Jill.

"Dad's shopping," says Amber, turning around. "Don't worry. It's on my list." She nibbles on a freshly washed carrot. Holding it up, she says, "Got these from Aunt Rebecca last week."

Thomas and Rebecca are more than Amber's family's farm friends. They are also her godparents.

"When was that?"

"Friday. I'm having supper there tomorrow too."

"You are?"

"Yes. Can you believe she's waiting until seven? I can't get there any earlier."

"She is?"

"Say! Wanna come? I can drive by and pick you up. I'd just have to phone and tell her I'll be half an hour later."

"I thought tomorrow night we might go grocery shopping together."

"Just give me your list, and Saturday after work, I'll pick everything up. What about supper at Aunt Rebecca's?"

"Sarah, Matt, and I are looking forward to spending time together, to catch up on things." Jill looks at Amber, hoping Amber might change her mind.

She has no idea that Amber is looking forward to hearing last-minute impressions about her father from Thomas. Amber hopes she might even find out where her father lives, at least in which city. Joseph spent last Friday night at Thomas and Rebecca's place.

"Bill will be there," adds Amber, hoping it will sway her mother. Removing an elastic band from her long blonde hair, she adjusts it so the ponytail sits higher up on her head.

Her hair's longer, observes Jill. *I hadn't noticed it before.*

"No, thanks." Jill nods, disappointed.

Jill's quick response leaves little doubt in Amber's mind that her mother's decision is final.

The next morning, Jill joins her children for breakfast. Conversation with Amber is short. In her old jeans, she rushes off to work. Sarah visits a little longer, but she too bikes off to work. Matt stays and talks about the friends he will see at the morning soccer practice. By nine thirty, Jill is home alone. Her feeling of being left out grounds her to the kitchen chair.

Her sadness is short lived. Gloria Brewster, Sunday school superintendent, phones. She asks if Jill is ready for company. Jill's affirmative answer is coupled with "But I have nothing to serve."

"No problem. I'm bringing two banana loaves."

"Two!"

"Yes. I'm also picking up Ellen, Ada, and Ruth. We are looking forward to seeing you. Just put on the coffee."

The visit from the Sunday school teachers takes up the rest of the morning.

In the afternoon, Jill finds that her hopes are once again out of step. Thinking that she should return to work soon, Jill calls her boss, Mr. Tarsen. She works as a receptionist for an insurance broker.

He asks her if she would mind waiting until September. During Jill's absence, he hired his daughter, who had just graduated from high school. She will be attending university in the fall.

Jill's initial thought is, *How would Amber feel if she were suddenly replaced?* Then she realizes that some of her physiotherapy appointments would be during work hours. While Mr. Tarsen wouldn't make an issue if she took time off, Jill knew he'd be better off with his daughter. She accepts his suggestion to return in the fall. His sigh of relief surprises her.

After Jill hangs up, she thinks, *I couldn't have gone to work anyway. I have no car.*

Buying a car scares her. She never bought one. Jill tries to recall what Joseph did. Her memories are vague. Impressions of test-driving the Impala cause Jill to miss Joseph. She shakes the pleasant memory out of her head. *What was I looking for? Comfortable, clean, easy to handle, easy to park. Must be more than that. Mileage! What's a good mileage?*

She wishes she paid more attention to what Joseph had said. Having a mechanic check the car puzzles her. *What does he look for anyway?* Then a disturbing revelation hits her. *I don't know any mechanics!*

She wonders if she should look for a vehicle in the newspaper or a used-car lot. Then Jill realizes she would need someone to drive her to the car lot. If it's a private purchase, she'll need a ride to the seller's house. *Amber maybe.* Amber's comments about her long days forces Jill to search for another person. Julie. *Julie will help. Sarah can babysit her kids while we go out.* Then Jill remembers that Julie works part-time too.

Beat up by the perceived complexity of buying a good vehicle, she considers a new one. *It should be really safe.*

As if Joseph were standing beside her, she imagines him shaking his head. *He never bought a new vehicle. Cost too much, he said.* Jill gasps. *No.* The thought of dipping into her nest egg, the one she set aside from selling the house, hits her with a force that causes her to shake her head. *I can't do that! It's the only savings I have. It's my only shield to protect me from poverty.*

Jill's already planned to withdraw money from her savings to cover expenses until she returns to work. Involuntary tightening of stomach muscles forces her to rush to the washroom and kneel before the toilet. While recovering, she rests her head on her arms over an open bowl. Comfort comes from remembering she survived her father, survived Dave's hunt for her, survived losing two babies. *I will survive Joseph's desertion.*

Jill stands up and pulls the towel to wipe the tears tracing down her face. She shuffles to the bed, defeated. Pulling the pillow to support her head and the blanket to her neck, she closes her eyes. The phone call to Mr. Tarsen creeps back. So does his request to come back in the fall. Too exhausted, she can't resist the flow of the afternoon frustrations, all coming from being without a vehicle. Hours seem to pass before she dozes off.

Matt and Sarah enter the apartment. Before Jill knows it, they are starting on supper. When she asks to help, they insist that she take it easy.

"But I'm not helpless," objects Jill.

"We don't want you to be too tired to visit with us tonight," offers Sarah.

Reluctantly, Jill accepts. The children clean up after supper too. She feels like she's still a patient in the hospital, a person needing care. *I thought that was behind me.*

As soon as their work is done, Sarah and Matt join Jill in the living room. Jill welcomes their stories. They fill in many gaps from her six-week hospitalization. Jill goes to bed content. *I'm part of the family, well, at least some of the family.* Before she falls asleep, she promises, *Tomorrow evening, Amber and I will talk.*

The following morning is a repeat of Friday, except a phone call comes after her children leave for their commitments. It's Eve, her daughter-in-law. "Can I and the kids come over?"

Jill looks forward to seeing her grandchildren. While their visit is a little more than two hours, Jill finds the pace of the children's activity and laughter draining. It's nothing like the peaceful hospital atmosphere. She doesn't object when Eve volunteers to make lunch for them before they leave.

Jill's afternoon nap is disturbed by a phone call. Mr. Tarsen apologizes. He confesses he allowed his love for his daughter to cloud his judgment. Linda, his daughter, pointed out she had no right to Jill's job. Her appointment was temporary. She expected that. It was okay with her if Jill wanted to return to work.

"Forgive me?" he asks.

"No problem."

"So when would you like to return?"

Next week is the first answer that pops into Jill's mind. Then she remembers she doesn't have a vehicle. The dread of shopping for a car sends a cold shiver down her spine.

"I don't think I'm ready to return yet," she begins. "Why don't I return in the fall, like we talked about before?"

Again, Jill hears relief in her boss's voice. For a moment, the discomfort of having no vehicle disappears.

After she hangs up, the prospect of purchasing a vehicle returns. So do the questions. *New or used? Dealership or private? What's a good vehicle? Who can help me?* The headache that started before lunch returns. She takes some Tylenol, pours cool water over a facecloth, squeezes it, and applies it to the back of her neck. It helps, but she decides she should lie down again. In hanging the cloth up, she misjudges evenly spreading it on the towel bar. It falls. With a quick reaction, she catches it but also knocks the toilet lid. The bang startles her. She jumps back, hitting her head on the bathroom door. The facecloth drops. Her confidence evaporates. *I need to rest.* She shuffles to her bed and pulls the covers over her head. Her eyes close.

Her sleep is short.

A low, deep male chuckle freezes her. She listens to a whispering. **"Can't run this time. Can you?"**

The accusation jerks her deeper into a nightmare. The urge to run from her tormentor prompts tight leg muscles. Nothing happens. Her legs fail to work.

"Can't run this time. Can you?"

The damning chuckle sparks a fighting spirit. "I *will* overcome this." Jill sits up, ready to face her challenger. Perspiration coats her face. Instinctively, she drags her feet to the bathroom sink and searches for the facecloth. Her failure to find the facecloth foreshadows her predicted future failures—failure to buy a car, failure to return to work, an overdrawn bank account, no children, no future. Exhausted, she returns to the bed.

A voice wakes her. Scrambling to grasp reality, Jill guesses she hears Amber from the kitchen. *She's home so soon. Oh yes. It's Saturday. The groceries.* Jill quickly manufactures a confident face and goes to see her daughter. Together, they put the groceries away.

Amber bides her time. She knows her brother and some boys from the church are painting the fence for the Boys and Girls Club. Sarah is at her part-time job. When the groceries are put away, Amber fires her first question.

"How did you get home from the hospital Thursday?"

"What do you mean how?" Jill buys time to consider her response.

"Just that. How did you get home? Who brought you?"

"A cab. Why?"

"Didn't Mr. Wynchuk offer you a ride?"

"I guess."

"You guess?"

"Okay. He did."

"And you didn't let him take you home?"

"Maybe I didn't want him to know where we live."

"Buuullshiiiit!" Amber's voice reaches two octaves above the tone of her previous question. She stretches her denunciation for even more effect.

"Amber! Your language!"

"What? You find it offensive? It stinks? I can understand that. It's like your last answer. It stinks. It stinks so bad I have to turn my face away." Her head turns so fast that her ponytail flies straight out.

"Amber, you're overreacting."

The cupboard door closes. Amber turns and says, "You expect me to believe you were worried Mr. Wynchuk would know where we live? Don't you think he was here visiting Dad and the rest of us while you were in the hospital? Come on!"

The news that Bill had been at her house catches her by surprise. It never occurred to her that Bill spent time with her family. "I thought he'd only phone."

"He helped us in so many ways. How could you? How could you ditch him?"

"For that very reason," Jill fires back, confident she is about to gain the upper hand. "He's done so much for us. I'll never be able to repay him. The worst thing I can do is add to my debt."

"Your debt? You think he was helping only you. Let me tell you—he was helping the whole family."

Amber reads Jill's surprise.

"Yes, the whole family, Sarah, Matthew, Daniel, me, and Aunt Julie."

"Really!"

"Julie couldn't take care of all of us so I got farmed out to Daniel. He and I fought. Then Dad came. Who do you think convinced Dad to come?"

"Daniel," Jill answers confidently.

"Wrong! Mr. Wynchuk. He talked Dad into coming back while you were in the hospital. Mr. Wynchuk said we all really need his help."

"Oh no." Shock racks Jill's response.

"So, you see, if there is a debt, then it is one that the whole family owes Bill, not just you. Right?"

Amber's pause forces a nod from Jill.

"But with Mr. Wynchuk, there is no such thing as debt. He's helping because he cares a lot for us. He expects nothing in return."

Amber sees and ignores Jill shaking her head in disagreement.

"Do you know he picked us up after you were in the accident?" Jill recalls asking the paramedic to call Bill after she failed to reach Julie, Joseph and Daniel.

Jill nods.

"Do you know he visited you almost every day when you were in the hospital?"

Because of Jill's anxiety she spent most of the six weeks in an induced paralysis.

"I heard something about that."

"And why do you think he was so attentive?"

"I don't know."

"Are you blind? Can't you see he loves you?"

"Don't be ridiculous. You're too young to know about love."

"He does. Who else would lavish so much attention on anyone?"

"You're too young to know about that kind of love."

"Really! Then why do you think he devotes so much time to you?"

"I told you. I don't know. But it's not love. I haven't given him any reason to love me."

"So I'm too young to know what's going on? And you're … you're too … too confused to know what's going on. How about Aunt Rebecca? Do you think she has a good grasp of reality? Would you trust what she says?"

Not knowing what else to do, Jill nods.

"She thinks Mr. Wynchuk is a lonely man."

"Nonsense."

"Ask her. I did."

"He has lots of friends in church and at the Wellness Center."

"Aunt Rebecca says since he lost his wife, he has no one whom he trusts to share his private thoughts, his hopes, his concerns with. Certainly the people at the Wellness Center wouldn't qualify. They have enough troubles of their own. Aunt Rebecca says he has a hard time sharing anything really personal. Only now, after Uncle Thomas and Aunt Rebecca have invited him for supper to their place several times, is he starting to open up."

"Sharing personal things? Like what?"

"I don't know. Aunt Rebecca wouldn't say. Has he ever shared anything really personal with you?"

Jill thinks back to the time when they were in Chicago. Revelations about being unable to help Donna, about being uncomfortable sitting by her still body surface.

Jill's nonanswer prompts, "He has. I can see it in your face. You see. He *is* lonely. He's looking for someone to love, someone to love him."

Jill shakes her head.

"Don't believe me? Then ask Aunt Rebecca. Those were her thoughts."

Jill leans against the counter as if she can't concentrate enough to keep her balance.

"And how did you treat him? He offered to drive you home. And you took a cab. You let him come for nothing." Pointing at her mother, she says, "You made him look like a fool."

"Hey! Where are you getting all this?"

"I told you Mr. Wynchuk came to Aunt Rebecca's dinner on Friday. He was hurt. I've never seen him so low. He told us you left before he got there. He learned you took a cab. It's like you didn't want anything to do with him anymore. He couldn't figure out what he'd done wrong. Uncle Thomas and Aunt Rebecca tried to lift his spirits, but they didn't really succeed. Mom. How could you be so mean? He's such a nice man."

"Amber, I've missed six weeks of my life. I'm still trying to get my bearings."

Jill looks at her daughter, who is expecting a reasonable explanation. She wants to say she needs time to adjust to the changes she's seen in the family. They're so unexpected. Adding the wrinkle of another person would be too much to handle.

No. Amber can't suspect I can't cope. Watching Amber's faith in her dissolve forces Jill to say, "Maybe I misread things." Jill hopes her confession dampens Amber's anger.

Pointing her finger at her mom, Amber says, "Then you should explain that to Mr. Wynchuk. Call him up. Apologize. Even invite him over for supper, like we used to."

"I don't know, Amber."

"Well, you better do something, because right now your actions are stinking up this whole place. You know ..." She pauses. "I really don't want to be in the same room with you right now. Maybe being at the fence-painting bee with Matthew will help me forget what I just heard from you. One more thing—I'm not too young to know about love."

Without waiting for a response, Amber grabs her purse and car keys and stomps out of the kitchen.

MENDING FENCES

"MOM, YOU COMING WITH us to Daniel's after church?" Amber zips up her backpack containing her riding clothes. Her invitation reflects what Joseph did when he stayed with them. They had driven to Daniel's after the worship service in the city.

Before the accident, Jill and her children attended the United Church. After the service, they frequently joined one of the families for lunch. Jill checks her purse for the weekly offering envelope. *With Amber going to Daniel's, she won't be here to ask me if I have talked to Bill.* Jill loses herself in yesterday's debate, a debate with no resolution.

After Amber left for the fence-painting activity, Jill wrestled with letting Bill back into her life. She admitted she enjoyed his company. Once, at the family conference, she admired the commitment he devoted to people. Stories of his work at the Wellness Center impressed her. No problem was too much for him, no person unreachable. From him, there was no halfhearted effort. *What a champion to have fighting for you,* she thought.

Then came her hospital roommate's remark. *I'd say he's more than just a friend. You're lucky to have such an attentive man.* While Mable's comment supports Amber's expectation that she phone Bill, it also does the reverse. *He's been visiting you almost every day that you've been in the hospital.* Jill felt like she was a client of his all-or-nothing attention.

No halfway measures with Bill. I can't handle that. Another man in my life! No. It's just too much.

Amber's perception of Bill's love for her challenges Jill's intent to avoid Bill. Then Rebecca's observation offers a ray of hope. Her *Mr.-Wynchuk-is-a-lonely-man* assessment gives Jill an idea. *I can begin to repay Bill for his visiting me in the hospital. I'll invite him for supper, for home-cooked meals. He'll like that. Yes, that'll work. I'll be repaying my debt.*

"Mom." Amber cuts into Jill's review. "Coming to Daniel's?"

Jill hears the invitation as if it were for the first time. The sound of her son's name triggers an instant reaction. "No." Daniel's sarcastic remark, "Children's education, Mom's prime interest," when he and the children came to visit her in the hospital still chafes her. *He can't stand me. I'd rather visit Ellen or Rachel or Gloria Brewster. They all came to see me when I was in the hospital.*

Shannon's stuffed Mr. Bear sitting on the fridge catches Jill's attention. She forgot to give it to Shannon when she was over yesterday. Eve's request—"Come and visit when you are able once you get out of the hospital"—causes Jill to reconsider seeing her city friends. *I can visit Gloria anytime. It's not often I can catch a ride to the country.*

Matt runs into the kitchen to join his mother and sister. The new baseball cap that his father bought him last week sits firmly on his head. He carries his baseball glove in a Safeway bag. Playing catch with Daniel after supper is one of his afternoon highlights. Sarah hurries after Matt with her riding clothes stuffed in a bag.

They're going with Amber!

"I'm coming," answers Jill, looking at her waiting daughter. She grabs the stuffed bear. Sarah offers the front seat to her mother.

During the drive to the United Church, tension gripped Jill every time she saw movement of a pedestrian or a vehicle. In spite of Amber's assurances that she had everything under control, Jill's feet frequently braced for an impact. For the drive to Daniel's, Jill sits in the back with her son.

Once Amber is on the highway, Jill hears, "Mom, I want to ask you for a favor."

"Yes, what is it, Matt?"

There is a long pause, and then her son looks at her. "I want you to call me Matthew. Dad said that's my baptized name. Amber and Sarah are already doing this."

"But I've always called you Matt. Why the change?"

"I like it. It reminds me of Dad. That's what he always calls me."

Silence fills the car. The hum of the tires on the road does little to distract the attention from listening ears in the front seat.

"I really miss Dad."

Jill sees sadness shade her son's normally bright face. *After only four days! That's all Joseph has been away.*

"Okay, Matthew. As you wish."

A smile lights up his face.

Sarah and Amber's front seat chatter once again fills the drive to Daniel's. Matthew turns to his mystery book. With nothing else to distract her, Jill adds her son's name change to other developments that have taken place during her convalescence. *Have I been stifling my children's growth?*

Her concerns vanish the moment her three grandchildren rush to the car door. A few minutes later, Daniel appears. He welcomes his guests for lunch. After lunch, as Jill expected, Sarah and Amber excuse themselves. They go to Martin Shopka's for their horseback riding.

Sharon and Shelly monopolize Jill's time. When Sharon brings a book for Jill to read, Jill notes that Daniel isn't around. He and Matthew escaped to the yard to play lawn darts and later catch.

Eve sees Jill is looking around for her son.

Laughing, she says, "Amazing how they fill everyone's time, isn't it?"

Jill agrees and plunges into reading Sharon's book. It reminds her of when she read to Daniel. Eve leaves to put Shawn down for his afternoon nap. When she returns, she makes tea and cuts some lemon squares for Jill. Eve's "go-and-play-with-Dad" sends Sharon outside. After the tea break, Jill enjoys talking and preparing supper with Eve.

During the silent ride home, Jill evaluates the afternoon. The reservations she had about visiting Daniel remain. Eve's acceptance of her is as caring as Sarah's or Amber's. Her grandchildren's loving attention surprises her. Jill guesses it is Eve's doing. A major plus is that Eve's mother, Gertrude, didn't join them. Jill believes Gertrude's microscopic eye would detect a saint's flaws.

Jill's thoughts return to Daniel. He was absent for most of the afternoon. *He can't stand being in my presence*, judges Jill. *His short appearance and politeness at lunch and supper fulfill a required hospitality role, probably one Eve insisted upon. A return visit isn't likely.* As the ride home continues, the prospect of not seeing Eve and the grandchildren haunts Jill. Her discomfort forces her to shift her position in the back seat. Back pain spikes. She gasps and then readjusts her position.

Looking for a less-stressful challenge, Jill's thoughts turn to Bill. Unlike Daniel, Bill accepts her just as she is. Being in his presence is relaxing. Amber's point that Bill is lonely no longer surprises Jill. She sensed that when she was in Chicago. It was one of the reasons why she chose to sit and talk with him on the restaurant balcony. His unexpected openness demonstrated a trust—an undeserved trust, she felt. She took Bill's revealing his feelings as a sign that he needed someone to talk to. By sharing her concerns about Bill with Joseph, she convinced him that they should invite Bill over for dinner. After only two dinners, a close friendship grew between Bill and her husband.

Amber's accusation, *How could you be so mean to such a nice man?* weighs heavily on Jill. To escape the crawling guilt, she turns her attention to a cramped feeling. Wedged in the back seat between the door and Matthew sleeping on her lap, she has little opportunity to move around. Slowly, she stretches her legs. Back pain seizes her. Jill chooses to endure the discomfort. *Suitable punishment for deserting Bill.* By the time Amber reaches their apartment, Jill decides she will phone Bill. *First, I must talk to Amber.*

The late arrival home sends everyone heading for bed, everyone except Jill. She won't fall asleep until she figures out what to say to Bill. Inviting him to dinner is easy. Explaining why she took a cab home from the hospital means some kind of admission. He could interpret it as her needing some help. She shakes her head.

The whistling kettle diverts her attention. By the time she pours the boiling water in her cup and waits for the tea to steep, her mind is on the good night hugs and kisses from her children. *No complaining.* Since they'd moved into the apartment, Sarah and Amber had had to share a room. Before, bickering frequently preceded bedtime. *I'll bet Joseph ended it. Maybe Amber has matured. Maybe it was better than sleeping at Daniel's.*

As she sips her tea, her thoughts turn to having missed an opportunity to talk to Amber tonight. *When do I catch her? Before she goes to work? Between six thirty and eight?* Worried that Amber may want to talk about her request, Jill dismisses the latter option. *Don't want to be responsible for*

Amber being late for work. Jill shakes her head. The tea isn't helping. *When she gets home for supper? Between nine and ten? After such a long day! She may be too tired.* Jill guesses she may have to wait until next weekend to talk about Bill. *But I should really phone Bill before then.*

Jill is finishing her tea when Amber comes padding into the kitchen for a bottle of water.

"Something wrong?" asks Jill, looking up at her daughter, who is wearing a housecoat.

"Can't sleep."

"Sarah talking?"

"Yes, but don't say anything to her. When Dad was here, we'd often talk. It's just that I have something I want to work out. I can't do that if she talks to me. I thought I'd come to the kitchen."

"Something I can help with?"

Amber doesn't want to tell Jill about her boyfriend. He hasn't returned any of her phone calls. Before final exams, they made plans for the next two years. He let her practice driving his car when she was taking lessons. They were so close.

Amber is sure that the disagreements about his driving habits didn't damage their relationship. She fears he's upset that she accepted working at the construction site. He preferred she work at the neighboring day care center. They'd have more time together. He was okay with her having to take a year or two to save up enough money to go to university. The possibility that Alex's last question was at the heart of their separation hurts Amber. *What's more important?* he said. *Being with me or going to university?* Amber said they could do both. She planned to drive from Edmonton to Camrose every weekend to see Alex. She thought that would satisfy him. Now she begins to wonder.

Why can't he be excited about me taking my art classes, like Mr. Wynchuk, like Dad? Why can't he be happy like Dad was when Mom took her correspondence courses? Maybe he doesn't love me.

The thought triggers memories of a conversation she had with Rebecca. Worried that maybe her parents might get a divorce, Amber asked her aunt in secret if her parents were still in love. Rebecca described many ways in which Joseph showed his love for Jill, including Joseph's support for Jill's drive to complete her education. Rebecca pointed out his stand wasn't popular in the church. Amber didn't know about Joseph's support for Jill teaching. Amber hung on to Rebecca's assurance that love was the glue that held her family together. *Love does exist.*

Alex's avoidance strategy has created a fissure in Amber's self-confidence. To counter her self-doubt, she clings to her mother's assurance: *You're special.* It's the centerpiece of her relationship with her mother. Amber's art teacher's recognition of her special talent and passion also bolsters her ego. Bill and the Wellness Center, through their sales and promotions of her paintings, second Jill's opinion that Amber is special. Joseph's boasting of Amber's paintings always draws a smile on Amber's face. In his eyes, she can see she is special. When Alex made extra efforts to find her, spend time with her, and applaud her painting, Amber felt it was unanimous. She *was* special.

Now his silence casts a shadow on Amber's glowing image. This has never happened. She feels flawed, like an incomplete painting. *I'm not worthy of Alex's love anymore.*

Amber's silence must concern Jill. Amber had always talked to her mother about her problems. "Amber?"

Recalling her mother's earlier offer, Amber fakes a smile. "No need." She grabs a bottle of water from the fridge and starts heading back to her bedroom, hoping Sarah will be in the mood to sleep.

"I'm thinking of phoning Bill tomorrow," begins Jill. She sips her tea.

Amber turns and faces her mother. Seeing she is serious, Amber says, "That's good."

"I'm planning on inviting him over for supper next Sunday. Now he might not be available or even want to come. If he does, can you be here too?"

"No problem."

"You sure? You and Sarah don't want to go horseback riding?"

"I'm sure. I could use some time to finish my painting. Sarah will understand."

"Then you can show it to all of us?"

"Yes. I only have to apply a sealant and let it dry."

Jill gets up and thanks Amber. She plants a kiss on her forehead. Amber takes a sip of her water, and when her mother disappears into her room, she sits at the table.

NEWS

KNOWING THAT BILL SERVES at the Wellness Center in the evening, Jill calls at lunchtime. She expects a cutting remark when Bill hears her on the line. It's not his nature, but she feels she deserves it. She's been home from the hospital for more than a week, and she hasn't called him to explain her quick departure. To her surprise, she receives a casual greeting. He politely inquiries about how she is adjusting to home life.

Jill admits that she was wrong to leave the hospital instead of waiting for him. No sooner does she begin with "I wasn't thinking clearly …" than Bill stops her.

"No need to explain. I thought you might want some time to adjust to being home, to talk with your children." His accepting attitude to her apology surprises her.

Jill is speechless. After he voices one of her prepared excuses, relief sweeps over her. Remembering the other reason for her phone call, Jill tells him that she and the children would like him to join them for supper next Sunday. She includes the children in the invitation because she thinks that Bill might not want to come if it is only her desire. She can't believe that Bill has no sore feelings about her deserting him. Still thinking that Bill will reject her offer, she has prepared herself to tell Amber that she tried.

Bill accepts her invitation.

After handling the toughest challenge for the day, Jill is ready for an uneventful afternoon. Her phone rings twice. Crystal and Ellen from Sunday school call. They each ask if they can visit the following afternoon. Jill's excitement gives way when she realizes she has no baking. With no car, she has no opportunity to run out and buy something. Gloria calls to visit too and solves Jill's problem. She offers to visit in the morning and bring some baking. The call that most excites Jill comes in the evening. It's from Julie.

"I'm back from holidays!" Julie salts her coming request. "Have I got news! When can I come over?"

"Like what?"

"For one thing, I saw your grandmother while I was in Ontario." Julie knows that information means she doesn't need to encourage Jill for an invitation. Jill fails to drag out a clue about Julie's news. They agree on early Wednesday afternoon. Julie budgeted the extra day to do some needed shopping.

Tuesday, after her Sunday school friends leave, Jill has nothing to do but speculate about Julie's news. Was it about Josey? Was it good or bad news? Could the news be about Julie's parents or Scott's? Why the secrecy?

The most that Jill can do to distract herself is talk to Matthew about entertaining his cousins when they come in the afternoon. Matthew's response is fast. "Tell Aunt Julie to bring the boys' bikes. We'll ride over to the school grounds and play soccer. Some guys are gathering to practice." Jill's promise of some money for treats is a bonus.

To impress Julie's children, Jill offers what's left of Gloria's blueberry shortcake. John Ryan and Jeff Roger's shouts of joy drown out Matthew's objection. He only had two pieces yesterday. By the time the water boils for tea, the boys are finishing their dessert and glass of milk. Between mouthfuls, Jill gathers Julie's children loved their holiday. Their highlights included going to a football game and fishing.

"Let's go, Number One!" shouts Jeff Roger as he shoves his chair from the table. They follow Matthew's lead.

After his brother's birth, John Ryan's nickname changed from JR to Number One. Number one for Julie's firstborn. Jeff Roger is Number Two.

"Nicknames," says Julie, laughing as Jill pours the tea. Julie scoops out the last of the blueberry dessert.

"So how were your holidays? Tell me all about them," says Jill, sitting down with her tea.

Without hesitation, Julie launches into the fun they had visiting her parents in Oshawa. Jill inquires about some of the places she remembers she used to go to. When Julie begins talking about Scott's parents, the joy disappears. Stories of how Scott's father's Alzheimer's affected his mother are disturbing. Julie's only good news is that the Wylers will be able to move into a new seniors assisted-living center at the end of September. The facility enables the patient and the spouse to live in the same building if not the same room. Scott plans to ask to work two shifts back to back so he can combine his time off to fly back to Oshawa mid-September to help his parents prepare to move.

"The children and I are going back with him," says Julie. "Why don't you come back with us?"

Instinctively, Jill responds, "Oh, I can't."

"Why not?"

Jill wishes she hadn't been so emphatic. She didn't want to tell Julie that she's afraid of bumping into Dave or Greg. And then there is her father. After all these years, she doesn't want to take the chance of bumping into him.

Scrambling for any excuse, she says, "Sarah will just be starting her senior high year. I should be around when she makes that change." Seeing Julie's slow nod and frown, Jill searches for a stronger defense. Then she remembers her job. "And Mr. Tarsen is expecting me back in September. He's been very patient with me. I've been off since mid-May. His daughter is covering for me, but she goes back to university in September. I must be back."

Julie's reluctant nod signals her acceptance, but her silence convinces Jill there is more.

"What?" asks Jill.

Julie looks directly into Jill's eyes. "Josey is now living in an assisted-living facility. It's her arthritis."

Because Jill hadn't seen her grandmother for about ten years she felt uncomfortable saying "Gramma." Sensing Jill's problem, Jill's grandmother said, "Just call me Josey."

Julie looks for and sees Jill's expected concern. "There is a walker in her room. The staff insists on it being there, but Josey refuses to use it. She insists on her cane."

"The one with a carved cat's head?"

"That's the one. A couple of the ladies on the staff half-threaten to hide it on her. They're concerned that one of these days, Josey's pain will be so great she'll fall and get hurt."

"Hiding her cane! I'll bet that doesn't go over well."

"It doesn't. Josey always keeps it in her sight. The staff member told me she even hides it under the sheets when she goes to bed."

Jill laughs. "I can see her do that." After a pause, she asks, "Is Josey in any pain?"

"When I was there, I didn't see it. At times, she moves very slowly. But one of the attendants pulled me aside. She told me there are times Josey refuses to go to the dining room to eat. The attendant guesses she's in too much pain. Later when she brings Josey supper, Josey eats."

"She takes painkillers?"

"Frequently."

"Sounds like things are becoming very difficult for her."

"They are. Are you sure you can't come down to see her?"

"Now? Yes. Maybe next year, during the summer."

"I'll tell her that when next—"

"I said maybe," Jill cuts in loudly and firmly. She regrets her sharp tone. Jill explains returning to Oshawa is something she never considered. "Given Josey's situation, it's now possible."

"It's not about the money, is it? Because if it is, Josey said she'd pay for everything."

"No," lies Jill. "I told you I have to be here for my children. And I have a job to return to." After Jill reiterates her excuses, she becomes suspicious. "Why would Josey be concerned about my financial situation anyway?" she asks. "What did you tell Josey about me?"

"She knows about your accident. And I told her that you were recovering. Remember? I saw you before I left."

"That doesn't have anything to do with financial troubles." Jill sees Julie fidgeting. "Is that all?" Jill leans forward, intent to find out what else Julie is hiding.

"You know you were in a coma for several weeks," pleads Julie. "I had to tell Josey that. If I didn't, she would never have forgiven me. And telling her you were conscious was good news. She needed to hear that."

Still working at the notion that Josey thinks she has financial concerns, Jill challenges Julie. "What else did you report? You didn't tell her I was divorced, did you?"

Leaning back as if to avoid being hit, Julie answers, "Yes, I did."

"You didn't!" Jill instantly blurts out.

She looks down ashamed. Her shortcomings are exposed to the most respected person in her life.

"I didn't have much choice, Jill. When you quit eating and I saw those pills on your night table—I really didn't know what to think. I needed help. I didn't want to turn to the pastor. If that came out in the church … I had to talk to someone."

"I can't believe it." Jill's words bounce off the floor.

"Josey told me if things didn't turn around soon, she would come down to see you. The only reason she didn't come immediately is because she knew how highly you value your privacy and solving your own problems. For a whole week, I had to keep her posted. Daily. When she was satisfied that you were on the mend, she said to call her only if I had any new concerns."

"How long have you been spying on me?" Jill refuses to look at her niece.

"Jill! That's not fair! We're not your enemies. We both love you. We just want to be there for—"

"How long?" Jill's demand clearly states she only wants to hear one more thing. Silence follows until Jill's eyes target Julie's forehead. "How long?"

Julie's answer comes as a whisper. "Shortly after Ann introduced us."

Jill turns away from Julie and shakes her head slowly.

I thought I could trust her. Everything I told her was in confidence. Jill continues to shake her head. Details she shared about Joseph and Daniel poke her like jabbing needles. *I can't trust anyone.* She stands up and corrects her conclusion, *Except Mary and Ann.* Jill begins to walk out of her own kitchen.

Julie says, "Josey made me promise not to say anything. It's only when I saw her last week that she said I should let you know she wants to help you. She knows what you are going through, and she can help you."

"Like she said, I'll handle my own problems." Her bedroom door closes.

Julie sits on the kitchen chair for another ten minutes, hoping Jill will come out. *How else could I have broken the news that Josey wants Jill to come down and see her? I thought once Jill knew that Josey knew of her troubles, there would no reason to try to keep hiding. We could have gone to see Josey together in September.*

Josey's advice returns to Julie. "Don't tell her that you've been updating me. Just ask her to come and see me." Julie understands now why Josey insisted on talking to Jill face to face. *It's the only way I'll be able to straighten things out with her.* Josey said she would like to come to Camrose, but she thought she couldn't handle it. That was the first time that Julie had ever heard Josey admit to not being able to do something.

As Julie steps out of Jill's apartment, she remembers something else she meant to share with Jill. *I forgot to tell Jill about her sister.*

Kathy very much wanted to see her sister too. She had volunteered to come back with Julie, but Josey vetoed it. She questioned how Jill would react. *Good thing too*, thinks Julie. She recalls Jill often talking as if she looked up to her older sister. Then there were times Jill demonstrated a fierce anger with Kathy for running away. *Jill might want to know that Kathy is happily married with two children, Joyce and Jack. Both are in postsecondary school.* After another moment, Julie guesses that Kathy's normal life might plunge Jill into despair. A comparison could be interpreted as another sign of Jill's failure.

Jill usually phones Julie every Friday morning. Julie waits until noon and then calls her cousin. To increase her chance of coming over for afternoon tea, Julie mentions that she saw Jill's sister in Oshawa. Jill's response surprises Julie. She shows an interest but no excitement.

For Julie, afternoon tea is awkward. While Jill is polite, she asks very few questions about Kathy, as if she really doesn't care. Julie feels like a social worker reporting on Jill's sister. Jill asks no questions about John Ryan or Jeff Roger or how Julie likes returning to work.

Jill's unexpected question is "Could you take me shopping? I have no vehicle yet. Company's coming on Sunday, and I would like to pick up a few things."

Julie forgot Jill has no transportation. The wording of Jill's question troubles her. Jill's question implies a strained relationship. "*Take me* shopping," she had said, not "*Let's go* shopping." Jill's vagueness catches Julie's attention. Buy what? Who is company? The openness that characterized their relationship is absent. Julie feels like she's being treated like an acquaintance.

Did telling Josey about the divorce cause this? Julie wonders how she can rebuild Jill's trust.

"No problem," says Julie casually. "When would you like to go shopping?"

"I won't be long," says Jill as they enter the cereal aisle in the co-op. Before Julie can comment, Jill rushes off to the produce area. She makes a few salad selections. After checking to make sure that Julie isn't near, she goes to the meat counter. Intending on impressing Bill, she selects a prime rib roast. Another quick glance around confirms Julie is nowhere around. When Jill arrives at the till, she chooses the line that is the farthest away from Julie even though it's much longer than the others.

As Jill walks to the car, she sees her niece sitting, waiting for her. Jill smiles and waves. "I really appreciate you helping me out like this," says Jill as she places her bag at her feet.

"Anytime," says Julie. She drives Jill home but isn't invited to go in with her.

Bill arrives at the apartment at four o'clock Sunday afternoon, the time Jill set. Jill notes his casual attire—sandals, short pants, and a *Love Orlando* T-shirt—a T-shirt he wore a couple of times when he visited her at the hospital. Bill joins Jill, Amber, and Sarah in the living room. Tea and homemade peanut butter cookies await them. For the first half hour, small talk allows them to catch up on events of the last week. Bill notes Amber glancing several times at her mother. Finally, he asks if he's interrupting something.

"You'll have to pardon Amber's impatience. I promised her she could show you her latest painting."

"Mo-o-om!" Amber objects to the characterization.

She prepared for tonight, thinks Bill. *No makeup, but every strand of hair is in its place.* Her bangs arch out and return to her forehead in a straight line. When they walked to the living room, he saw her straight, below-the-shoulder-length blonde hair hang down, the bottom ending in an even line across her back. *Jill must have cut it for her*, he thought.

"Go ahead, Amber." Jill pulls at Sarah's arm, wanting her to help her in the kitchen. "We've already seen Amber's masterpiece, so if you don't mind, Sarah and I'll check on supper. I expect Matthew to be home before too long. Then we'll eat."

As her mother and sister leave, Amber reaches to the side of the love seat and pulls out a towel-draped frame. She sets it on the love seat beside her and uncovers her work. Amber glows after seeing Bill's surprise.

"It's beautiful!"

"It's for Dad," offers Amber. "I wanted to finish it for him before he left, but I just didn't have the time."

"For your dad?"

"Yes. This is the weeping birch on our old farm. He says he planted it the year his uncle Mike died. When we were at the farm a few weeks ago, Dad couldn't stop admiring it. Do you see Dad in here?"

Bill looks at the painting. "The shadow." He points to a partial dark shadow cast on the lawn at the bottom of the frame.

"That's right." Amber points to the oak tree to the left of the birch tree. Only a few branches reach into the scene. "Dad's uncle planted that tree right after he bought the farm. The weeping birch represents Dad keeping his uncle Mike company."

"He loved his uncle," murmurs Bill.

"That's why the tears," explains Amber. She points to the water droplets hanging from the leaves on the trees. "It comes from the sprinkler down here. The arc of the spray makes a perfect sad face." Amber traces the spray line. "When I stood beside Dad, the droplets reflected the sun's rays. To Dad, it seemed like the tree was crying."

"How did you do that?" Bill points to the sparkling droplets.

"A very small brush to form the tears. Then, using a toothpick, I touched each droplet with a dab of glue. While the glue was still damp I slid very small sparkles across the scene. Later, so the sparkles wouldn't fall off, I applied a light sealant."

"That must have taken a long time."

"Hours and hours. It was worse than working on a thousand-piece puzzle."

"This is awesome!"

"Only one problem. What do I call it? I thought of *Mike* or *Uncle Mike*. What do you think?"

"Not bad. Are you planning to give it to your father?"

"Yes."

"Then it will make sense to him."

"For others who see it, the title won't have much meaning." Amber shrugs.

"And I'm sure your dad will want to show this off."

"That's what I was thinking too. How about *Misses Me*? That's what Dad said when he saw the tree after it had been watered. Uncle Mike misses me."

"That's perfect. Where do you come up with these great ideas?"

"Ideas?"

"Ideas for your painting?"

"Being observant. I hear a person talk about something that moves them. Then I try and capture it in color. Dad inspired this painting. My next one comes from something I heard Mom talking about this afternoon."

"Really! What?" Bill leans forward, anxious to hear Amber's observation.

"Mom was showing me the pictures from a photo album that Aunt Julie brought from my Mom's grandmother. At first, Mom talked about the flowers, memorizing their names. Then her attention switched to the solid square redbrick pillars, sun tanning on a wide balcony, listening to the birds and a wind chime. She said the chimes sounded like angels singing her to sleep. Just listening to how she talked, it sounded like she'd drifted back, like she could fall asleep on that balcony. I got the feeling she wishes she were there now. I'm going to try to catch her homesick feeling in my next painting."

"A lot of that sounds like what we saw in Chicago. There was a restaurant that had a balcony. Your mom and I sat on it until the sun went down. And I believe there was a wind chime too."

"I don't know anything about that."

"Any idea how you will go about tackling this project?"

"At this point, I only have some impressions. I have to figure out how I'll work them into the painting."

"Impressions? Like what?"

"Mom talked a lot about the red brick. I don't know why that's important, but I feel I have to have it in the painting. You know she said the brick in the house we just sold had the same kind of finish?"

"Really!" Bill suspects he's glimpsed a bit of something special in Jill.

"Also, I have to have a view from above and outside the balcony, a balcony that must be on the second floor. Listening to Mom, I could almost hear her say *safe enough to close my eyes*. Mom talked of a lounger, or a person on it. And, of course, I *have to have* the wind chimes. Anyway, I have a lot of planning to do." Amber reaches across and catches Bill's hand. When he looks at her, she says, "Don't breathe a word about this painting to anyone. I haven't told Mom. It's to be a surprise, but I don't know when I'll finish it."

Bill's exploration of Amber's project is cut short by a dinner call. Neither Bill nor Amber hears Matthew come in. When everyone sits at the table, Amber leads in prayer. Then everyone digs in. Bill eats so much of the roast beef, baked potato, peas, and carrots that he easily agrees to dessert later, much to Matthew's disappointment. Jill's brownies have been on his mind since yesterday afternoon.

"I think I could use a little after-dinner walk," says Bill. "Get rid of some of the calories." He looks to see if Jill will accept the invitation.

"Great idea," says Amber. "Mom, why don't you and Mr. Wynchuk go? Matthew and I will clean up. Right, dear brother?" Amber fixes her look on Matthew. He knows not to object.

"You sure?"

"We're sure, Mom. Go."

Once they're outside, Jill says, "There's a playground about four blocks from here. It's like a park, a perfect place to relax."

Jill sets an easygoing pace, a pace like they had when they were strolling through the hospital gardens. She's in no hurry to return home. Her hope is they'll talk freely like they did when they walked around the hospital gardens. Silence accompanies them for the first block.

To end the impression that Bill is studying her with psychologist's eyes, she struggles to find something to question him about. Nothing new comes to mind. From the lively conversation before supper, she learned about Bill's clients at the Wellness Center and the work he is doing in his yard.

"You in any pain?"

At the sound of Bill's voice, relief sweeps over Jill. By the way he asks, she believes he's concerned, not trying to make conversation. Afraid silence will return after she answers his question, she briefly considers admitting to some pain. Heading back would naturally follow. *I'll reject that option. I must find out if I damaged our relationship, the relationship we built during Bill's hospital visits.*

"Some," admits Jill. "But the pills I took at supper should kick in soon."

"If you want to head back—"

"No. Walking is good for me. I haven't done much of that lately."

They cross the street.

"Because?"

"I don't know," Jill lies.

She doesn't have any one to walk with. Julie has been on holidays. Since Jill discovered that Julie wasn't the friend she thought, she guards what she says. The information could get back to her sister or her grandmother.

"I ask because you are fairly quiet today."

Jill says nothing.

"I expect that you're happy now that you're home."

She wants to say yes, but she knows Bill will detect she's not being truthful. She hates being so transparent, at least to him.

"Kind of." Jill gazes down the street, hoping he doesn't see any sign of her disappointment with Julie.

"I remember when you were in the hospital, you said you missed the daily contact with your children. Now you see them every day. Is that turning out to be a problem?"

Jill stops by the curb and faces Bill. "It's different now. We see each other at meals and in the evenings, but things are different. The children have created new lives for themselves. Matthew is off playing soccer, doing odd jobs, at the show with his friends. Sarah has a part-time job. Some evenings, a couple of Sarah's friends from the Community Drama League drop by to drive her to practice. And Amber. She works those ridiculously long days. I have to get up early to see her at breakfast. Then she comes home so late. All she has time for is supper and going to sleep. I think she would like to paint, but I never hear a complaint. We've been apart so long, you know, while I was in the hospital, I wonder if she feels we can't talk."

"You're not a part of your children's lives like you were."

"Yes!" Jill's happy to hear Bill voice her feelings perfectly. No hint of judgment.

"A premature empty nest feeling."

"Exactly!" Jill continues as they turn toward the park. A smile lights up her face.

During the last week, she had been whipping herself with the notion that she was being selfish wanting her children around the house like they always had been. Bill's words, *empty nest*, remind her that Rebecca had complained about the same thing when her children moved out of the house.

It's normal, thinks Jill. Her pace slows as they enter the park. Bill's *premature* captures Jill's attention. Someday, Jill realizes, all her children will move out. She'll be alone. *Is Bill trying to tell me to prepare for that?* As Jill continues her walk, the idea of being alone bounces back. Her stomach muscles tighten in anticipation of being hit. *Being alone. That's not normal. Rebecca has Thomas. Mary has Ed. Ann has Pete.*

She wraps her arms around herself as a cool breeze blows through her light cotton T-shirt. *Wish I'd taken my sweater.*

Bill's voice cuts into her deliberations. "Something else wrong?"

The question sounds more like a statement, a statement based on an observation.

"No." After Jill answers, she suspects Bill knows she isn't being truthful. She regrets he can read her so easily.

A light touch on her shoulder stops her. She faces Bill. He nods ever so slightly as if to confirm his earlier observation.

Turning away, Jill says, "What makes you think so?"

Without hesitating, Bill says, "When we started our walk, you were in machine mode. You stared straight ahead, ignoring everything around you. In the last block, you glanced at the squirrel scrambling up the tree and looked at the kids yelling in the yard. You even waved to the fellow watering his flower bed. When we entered the park, you returned to machine mode."

Jill nods. No denying Bill's observations. Not wanting to talk about being alone, she searches for another topic.

"Remember I said being limited to the hospital grounds was like being in a kind of prison?" She continues her walk.

Bill nods.

"Being home is only a little better. If I want to go anywhere, I have to rely on a cab."

"So-o-o. Call me. I'll drive you anywhere you want."

Jill looks at him to see if he is serious. She shakes her head. "Without a car, I'm not free to book my physiotherapy appointments. And then in September, I'll have to have some way to get to work."

"Then buy a new car or at least a replacement car."

"The insurance settlement hasn't come through yet, and it won't for some time, unless I sign a waiver about my back. I don't intend to do that until the doctor tells me to."

"Good. But you don't have to wait for the settlement to buy a car. You sold the house. That should leave you with a sizeable nest egg."

"I can't." Jill's response is immediate. She looks at Bill as if daring him to challenge her.

"Borrow from your nest egg. Replace it when the settlement comes through."

"If it comes through."

"It will. Don't worry."

"That money is for special circumstances, emergencies."

"And this isn't?"

"Well, I guess. Certainly by September it will be."

"Sooner, if you want to take your therapy."

"Going to check out a vehicle isn't easy. I haven't a car to drive there."

Jill recalls waiting for Julie to return from her holidays. She thought the two of them would go looking at cars, but that was before she learned that Julie reports everything back to Josey. Hoping that she might catch Amber with some free time, Jill had been checking the paper to see what private deals were available. A private deal would be cheaper, she thought. Determining if a car is good or not is still a problem.

"Need help? Call me. Like I said before, it would be my pleasure."

Jill's expression shows Bill that she is considering his offer.

"Is Amber happy with her vehicle?"

"Yes. Why?"

"I helped her find hers. If you like, I can help you find yours."

"Well." Jill struggles with cashing in a part of her savings.

"Then it's settled."

Jill looks at Bill and smiles. "Thank you."

First time I've seen her accept help without thinking how she would try to repay it. Bill returns her smile.

As they walk through the park, Jill describes what she wants in her vehicle. Bill lists the things as an owner that she'll have to do. Satisfied that her transportation problems are on the verge of being solved, she turns her attention to nature's summer display. Together, they name shrubbery, comment on work that the gardeners need to do. Their wandering brings them to two families gathered around a small fire. Jill recognizes the children. They're in one of the Sunday school classes.

Bill and Jill join them. Bill notes an energy and joy in Jill's conversation, especially when she talks about the freedom to be involved in life that her new car will give her. Her list of missed activities includes dropping in to see Sarah at her part-time job, watching Matthew at some soccer games, and rejoining the drama club. "It's like I get my life back again," she says, laughing.

As she and Bill walk back to the apartment, she shares stories about the neighbors in the area. Jill stops and talks to some children playing in the street. Only when they reach Bill's car does Jill tell Bill how much she enjoyed the walk in the park and sitting by the fire. They stir memories of times she and Joseph spent on the farm.

"Then I take it we can do this again next Sunday?" Bill presents an uncertain face.

Looking at him, Jill laughs. "If you're fishing for another invitation, you have it."

As Bill prepares to drive away, he thinks, *I can't remember when I've seen Jill look so happy.*

SHOPPING FOR A CAR

THREE DAYS LATER, BILL phones Jill, reaching her after supper. Her interest in buying a car has motivated him to check with people around him.

"Hey, Jill. I've got good news. I found two people who are interested in selling their cars. You interested in checking them out with me?"

"Just checking." Fear of selling some of her investments has caused her to again question purchasing before the insurance settlement comes through.

"Good enough. Can you free yourself late Saturday afternoon?"

"Saturday! Not Sunday afternoon?"

"One of the sellers is a widow from my church. She won't do business on a Sunday."

"Okay."

"I'd also like to arrange for you to see the second car too. That owner doesn't live too far away from the widow. The guy is a friend of a friend. I know he takes good care of his vehicles. If we see both vehicles, that would probably mean that you would be home too late to prepare supper, so I was thinking we could go out for supper. What do you think? My treat."

Bill expects an excited yes. He's greeted by silence. Her mumbled "I suppose" puzzles him.

"Pardon me?"

"Sorry," says Jill quickly. She realizes she's thinking out loud. "I'm just figuring out what I could leave for the kids for supper. Anyway, yes. There's some leftovers in the fridge."

The first car that Jill takes out for a test drive is a white Malibu. Afraid that the car's price might prejudice her, Jill asks Bill not to tell her the asking price until after the test drive. The eight-year-old car handles well, but that's not why Jill drives it for twice as long as Bill expects. The revived pleasure of being free to go anywhere she wants whenever she wants convinces her she wants a car soon. Prompted by the next appointment Bill asks that they return the Malibu. Disappointed, Jill heads back. Jill's half-hour drive seems like only five minutes.

Bill waits until she parks the vehicle before telling her the price. Upon hearing the cost, she tells herself to forget it. It's more than twice what she hoped to spend. Jill tells Wilma, the owner of the car, that they will get back to her after looking at a few more possibilities.

The second vehicle is a silver Impala. It is a year older than the Malibu and twenty-five hundred dollars less. Even before Jill learns the price of the car, she falls in love with it. An Impala is the first car Joseph bought for her. The familiarity of the instrument panel, the car's handling, and the price makes this her first choice. She only takes a ten-minute drive before she returns it to Mr. Cardeski, the owner. With a little prodding from Bill, the owner indicates he is willing to cut his price by five hundred dollars. Jill is set to buy the car. Then Bill echoes her earlier words—"We'll get back to you after looking at a few more possibilities."

Jill can hardly wait until they are out of sight of Mr. Cardeski's house before she questions Bill. He reminds her of their afternoon purpose, research. As they approach the restaurant, he promises they will talk about it at dinner.

As soon as the waiter takes their order, Jill says, "Okay, tell me why I need more research. You know I was satisfied. I wanted it, especially after Mr. Cardeski cut his price."

"You're right. I knew you would be interested in buying that vehicle."

Jill's mouth drops at his admission. Bill raises his hand to prevent Jill from challenging him. His action reminds her of Joseph.

"You remember one of the things you said when I picked you up? You said we are only going out to look at vehicles, not to buy any. Do you remember?"

"Yes, but—" Bill's hand shoots up again.

"I can imagine the pleasure of driving again excites you. You just can't wait to get a car."

Jill nods, wishing Bill couldn't read her so well.

"And that's why I told Mr. Cardeski that we would get back to him. I thought that when your emotions settled down, you would appreciate time to think about your choices, maybe discuss them with Julie."

"Yes. Julie and I are going shopping, grocery shopping next week. I can talk to her about the cars then."

"And I might know of another vehicle. I'm waiting for the guy to get back to me."

Before their dinner comes, Bill leads Jill in an evaluation of each of the vehicles. He makes notes about each car in his coil ring pocket book. In considering the Impala, Bill points out that it has thirty thousand more miles on it. He suggests that while that is a good reason for its lower price, it could also mean more repairs.

Jill admits that she didn't think of that. Her first car, the Malibu, has less chance of problems. When their food comes, they agree to see other cars next Saturday. Bill adds, "And go out for dinner?"

Jill insists dinner will be on her. Before they leave the restaurant, Bill tears out the sheet with his notes from his notebook and gives it to Jill so she can use it when she talks to Julie.

The following Saturday, after Jill and Bill order their food at the Norseman Restaurant, Jill confesses none of the vehicles that she saw at the Buick dealership impressed her. While the prices were in the range of the Malibu, they all had substantially greater mileage.

"Did you talk to Julie about last week's cars?"

A frown crosses Jill's face. "Yes."

"And?"

"She recommended the Malibu. She pointed out the inconvenience of bringing the vehicle to the dealership for repairs."

"Yes."

"She also said since there will only be Sarah and Matthew at home, I don't need a large car." Jill shakes her head. The familiarity of the Impala still holds a strong attraction for her. It reminds her of a much easier life.

"I still would like to look around a little more. Next time, let's see the

Toyota dealership? Julie says I should look at their vehicles. They may have better mileage."

"No problem. Dinner again? My treat." Jill's pause causes him to add, "My turn." He smiles.

Jill nods and reflects his smile. "If I didn't know any better, I'd think you like hunting for cars just so we can go out for dinners."

Bill sips his tea as he watches Jill's reaction. "Don't worry. I hope you'll make a decision next week. Too many options clutter one's head."

The waiter brings their order.

"Having a meal out makes me feel like it's a special occasion. Know what I mean?"

"I do. I have that same feeling when you serve me your delicious home-cooked suppers."

As Jill digs into her fish and chips, she asks Bill if he could drive her to her physiotherapy appointment on Wednesday. She explains that Julie is working that afternoon, and it was the earliest appointment she could get. Bill agrees.

The next Saturday, after going to the Toyota dealership, Bill and Jill dine at Eastside Mario. Jill's poker face leaves Bill guessing. Did any of the cars appeal to her? He suspects she likes the first car the salesman showed her. He started with the price range she had in mind, and he presented her with a black ten-year-old Corolla. After the test drive, she asked for a newer model, suggesting she wasn't satisfied. The next car, a navy Corolla, was a seven-year-old vehicle and priced the same as the Malibu. She took it for a short drive. When she returned, the salesmen, thinking Jill's desires were flexible, convinced her to drive a three-year-old Corolla. Upon returning it, Jill thanked the salesmen for his time and told Bill it was time to leave. As Bill drove, she gave no clue as to her reactions. From her abrupt departure, Bill thinks none of the cars interest Jill. Because the first car fit her price range, he guesses it is a possibility.

Unable to contain his curiosity Bill asks which vehicle interests her the most. Her response, "We'll talk at the restaurant," doesn't help. He tries again by asking if she is ready to make a decision tonight. She heightens his curiosity by saying, "I think so." Like they did the first car-shopping afternoon, Bill waits until the waiter takes their order. Then he asks Jill about the cars she saw this afternoon.

Jill looks at Bill for a minute. She says nothing. Digging in her purse, she pulls out the notepaper he gave her about the Impala and Malibu.

"I suppose you know that these two …" She holds up his slip of paper. "… are the yardstick by which I measured all the vehicles since."

"Even the Ford I showed you after your physio?"

"Yes. And I'll admit the first car I took out today for a drive is tempting. When I saw the mileage, it was three times greater than the Malibu's. I ruled it out." She smiles as she sees Bill's approval. "And the second one, the one that costs the same as the Malibu, well, its mileage was quite a bit more. If I had to choose between those two, then the Malibu would win."

"So we're back to the Malibu or the Impala?"

"Yes."

"And?"

"Like I told you before, I'm partial to the Impala. I know you and Julie think I should take the Malibu, but three thousand dollars' difference is too much to ignore. It could cover a lot of repairs if the need should arise." She pauses for a moment and then continues, "I don't suppose you could get Wilma to reduce her price?"

"Wilma has a small pension. Her husband was a businessman and invested in the company instead of a pension plan. The sale of the car is an attempt to rebuild her diminishing nest egg."

Jill imagines she could be in that situation too if she doesn't watch her spending. "Oh! I didn't know. In that case, don't bother. Besides, there's no guarantee that the Malibu won't come up with unexpected repairs."

Bill worries Jill might have car trouble on the highway, maybe when she travels to Edmonton to visit Amber or Ann and Pete. *If it happens in the winter …* He shakes his head, not wanting to think what would happen.

Jill sees Bill shake his head. "There's only a year difference between the two. You don't think it's possible that the Malibu would have any major repairs?"

Bill considers offering to cover the difference in the price between the two vehicles, but he knows Jill wouldn't accept it. *She's too self-reliant.*

"Bill?" Jill waits until he acknowledges her. "You don't think it's possible that the Malibu would have any major repairs?"

A solution flashes through Bill's mind. He smiles and says, "No. As a matter of fact, I would be willing to bet on it."

"And if the Malibu does break down, then what?"

"I'll pay for the repairs. Remember. That's repairs, not maintenance."

He threw the clarification in so Jill wouldn't think he was trying to compromise her independence.

"You're that sure?"

"Yes. And if you buy the Malibu and nothing goes wrong in the first year, what are you willing to put up?" Bill smiles, seeing the tables turned.

"What do you want?"

"Since there is a year's difference between the two vehicles, I would like your promise that for the next year, you will treat me to your terrific Sunday home-cooked dinners."

"I'm already doing that."

"Then you have nothing to lose. I have the confidence and pleasure of those meals and your company."

"You don't make a very good deal for yourself, you know? But I'll accept. Tell Wilma I'll close the deal on Monday, if you're still willing to chauffeur me around for one more day."

Bill agrees. He calls the waiter over and orders a glass of wine. "To celebrate," he says. A second glass of wine follows after the meal.

"How would you like to take me to a party?" Jill looks at Bill, knowing she's snagged his curiosity. She brings a cup of tea and brownies, part of their Sunday afternoon routine. They usually spend half an hour catching up on events of the week, and then Jill prepares supper.

"What party? Where?" Bill pours himself a cup of tea.

Jill explains that Matthew's birthday falls at the end of the month and Sarah's is early in September. The last Saturday in August, Amber moves to Mary and Ed's.

"So Mary suggested that on Saturday afternoon, we celebrate Matthew's and Sarah's birthdays and Amber's starting university at their place. Sarah and Matthew are looking forward to it. Pete and Ann said they'd come. Eve loves the idea. It gives her a chance to do some shopping at West Edmonton Mall in the morning. Scott's home, so Julie says her family can come too."

"I didn't think Mary's place is large enough for all these people."

"She's reserving the common room if all the family is coming. So far, the only ones who can't make it are Thomas and Rebecca."

"Yes, I remember," says Bill, cleaning his silver-framed glasses on his shirt. "I think that's their church's new year kickoff. Rebecca is one of the ladies in charge of organizing the meal. Thomas and Martin Shopka are in charge of barbecuing. For that day, Thomas convinced Mark Swesson to take his place at the farmer's market.

"Lately, Mark has been there helping Thomas," continues Bill. He takes a large bite of his brownie. "You know, Thomas is seventy-one. He's finding it difficult to set up for the market. The last two Saturday mornings I dropped by and helped him. Closing isn't so bad. He has less produce. I told him one day he'll have to give it up. He hates to. He'll miss his customers. They're his friends. He'll also miss the other vendors. He knows the life history of most of the regulars. I suggested finding someone else to share his kiosk like he did with Joseph. He liked it. That's how Mark came into the picture."

"Aren't you a fountain of information! Where did you get all that from?"

"Usually every second Friday, I come to their place for dinner. And I'll tell you something else, just between you and me?" He waits for Jill to nod her agreement. "Rebecca has already asked me to talk to Thomas about giving up the market. She says he comes home very tired."

"I'm sure it will be hard for Thomas," agrees Jill.

"Now, about your party."

"Yes. Will you be able to make it?

"No problem."

"Good. Do you mind driving? I've never driven in Edmonton. I'm afraid I'll get lost."

"I can, but wouldn't you like to show off your car?"

"You can drive it there."

"Or you could drive and I'll navigate."

"I like that. In the future, I'll be more prepared to handle it myself." Then she adds, "That is if you aren't able to come with me."

Bill pours himself a second cup of tea and admires Jill as she goes about preparing supper. Energy and confidence mark her actions. At first, he credits her having a car for her positive outlook. Thinking of the upcoming party, he realizes her involvement in her children's lives has made the big difference.

Bill recalls Jill reporting about Sarah's dress rehearsal. She was so proud. Sarah received so many compliments on her supporting role. Jill proudly announced that next weekend there were three shows. She'd already convinced Matthew to come to the Saturday performance.

She asked me if I was coming. It was like I'm part of the family, Bill thought.

When he accepted, Jill invited him to dinner on Saturday, saying it was a bonus. She promised it didn't take the place of his Sunday dinner.

JILL'S RECONCILIATION

JILL AND BILL WALK along a familiar park path. She enjoys their regular Sunday walks. Poplar leaves from a nearby tree catch her attention. The yellow soaks into the disappearing green.

"You're unusually quiet today," says Jill.

Bill nods but doesn't explain.

"Something important on your mind?"

"You could say that." Bill's voice is low, as if he's uncertain if he should say anything.

"Want to talk about it?" She suspects it's about the friend that he is going to visit for a week.

Bill points to a picnic bench. They sit down. He turns to her and holds her hands. Then he looks around to see if anyone is nearby.

"Last week, at the party in Edmonton, you seemed to have a lot of fun."

"I did."

"Yes. I saw you laughing and talking with just about everyone, Ann and Pete, Mary and Ed, Julie and Scott. You really enjoyed playing with your grandchildren, especially Sharon, Shelly, and Shannon."

"I did."

"I had a chance to talk with Eve. She said she's happy that you phone her weekly."

"I like her. She's easy to talk to."

"Interesting. She told me you've only been over to their place once since you came out of the hospital. She thinks it has something to do with an unresolved issue with Daniel. The fact that you hardly talked to Daniel at the party worries her. Is there a problem?"

Jill's first reaction is to get up and walk away, to not answer Bill's question. His grip on her hands prevents her from leaving. She suspects that he's deliberately holding her so she will not escape. The gentleness with which he holds her hand suggests permission to leave, permission to avoid dealing with his probing if that's what she really wants.

Guessing that Bill wants to help her, Jill chooses her words carefully. "I think he blames me for the divorce." She looks down.

"So this is a short-term problem, a recent development?"

Jill wonders how much more Bill knows about her strained relationship with Daniel. She looks up and finds him studying her closely. *Got to be completely truthful. If I don't, he will see it in my eyes. He always does.*

"No. We've never been really close."

"And you're comfortable with this?"

"No. Of course not. But there's nothing I can do about it."

"And if there is, would you be willing to try?"

"Yes."

Jill's quick, firm response convinces Bill she's sincere.

"I might have an idea." He pauses, afraid to touch what he understands is a festering sore.

"Well?"

Bill looks at Jill's serious face. "You know in the Bible we're instructed to confess our sins." He paraphrases the first and third verses in Psalm 32. "The person who confesses their sins is blessed. The weight of the past mistakes doesn't become an unbearable burden."

"I should ask Daniel for forgiveness?"

"To start the healing process, yes."

"If I remember the Bible reference correctly, it refers to confessing sins to the Lord."

"And I would suggest that applies to personal relationships too. When the Bible refers to bones wasting away, if you don't confess your sins, I would say that's what is happening with your ties in Daniel's family."

"You're stretching it."

"Then how would you describe your relationship with Daniel's family? You know, I hear you talk a lot about what Amber, Sarah, and Matthew are doing or how they feel. I never hear you talking about your grandchildren. You've said you phone and talk to Eve, your daughter-in-law. I haven't heard you say you phone and talk to your son. It sounds like you care very little about Daniel."

Jill yanks her hands free. "That's not fair. You're making more of this than is the case."

"Then why is that Eve has the same impression as I do? She says Amber and Sarah call more often than you do. She guesses you call out of some feeling of obligation."

"She told you that! Why doesn't she talk to me about Daniel?"

"She said she's tried to talk to Daniel, but he isn't very forthcoming. She's afraid of the same result with you. It's even worse. She's afraid if she brings up her concern with you, then her relationship with you will be broken."

"So what am I to confess? I haven't done anything wrong." Jill slides a few inches away from Bill.

"In your mind, no. There must be something or things that you did that really bothered Daniel. He either disagreed with it or didn't understand. You need to think back to when you and Daniel began growing apart. See if you can identify what may have caused it."

"And what if I can't figure out what is bothering him?"

"Take your time. Think about it. Come up with possibilities. What's important is that Daniel can see that you're trying, that you want to fix things up. From what I saw at the party, I have the impression you really want to have more involvement with your grandchildren. Right?"

"Yes."

"Mend your relationship with Daniel. Then you'll feel more comfortable phoning and visiting your grandchildren. All I ask is that you think about what I said. When I come back, we'll talk about it."

"Come back?"

"Yes. Wednesday, I'm off to speak at a conference and visit a friend. I'll be gone for about a week."

"I think we should be heading back," says Jill. She stands up.

As they walk back to Jill's apartment, she is quiet. She wishes Julie would be around longer so she could get her reaction to Bill's idea of asking for forgiveness. Maybe Julie could even help her figure out what she did that got under Daniel's skin.

Julie, Scott, and the children leave for Oshawa in two days. Scott will be helping his parents move. Jill offered to take care of Julie's children so they could attend school, but Julie insisted on taking them with her. She wants John-Ryan and Jeff-Roger to see their grandfather before his memory deteriorates too much. Julie said being with family is more important now than going to school.

Jill looks ahead and sees the apartment parking lot. Bill's car is in the visitor stall. It occurs to her that he may leave for home right away. She's afraid her silence could be interpreted as anger. They can't part that way. She needs to know that if she asks Daniel to forgive her, Bill will be by her side. *I can't face Daniel on my own. He could have a long list of grievances.*

She invites Bill up for tea. During her walk back, she couldn't think of any event that would irritate Daniel. To give her time to work up the courage to admit that she couldn't guess what might be bothering Daniel, she counts her ten peanut butter cookies one by one. Sitting down, she says, "There are always things a parent needs to tell a child to do that they won't like. Those are petty things. Nothing could have had a lasting effect. A child should do what a parent tells them to. A parent knows best. Right?"

"Right," says Bill confidently. "And Joseph would have supported you on that. So, was there anything about how to raise Daniel that you and Joseph disagreed on?"

"You know, it's been so long ago. Even if I do come up with something, I doubt it will do any good."

"Leave an issue unresolved, and you leave an open window for the devil to turn people against you."

"I don't know." Reluctant to follow Bill's idea, Jill shakes her head.

"It's worth a try. Trust me." Seeing Jill's silence, he asks again, "You *do* trust me?"

Bill's question opens a wound that Jill tries to ignore. *My friend, the one I met in Chicago, the one I trusted, the one who sided with Joseph when Joseph said he wanted to divorce me.* Jill recalls Joseph's words, "Even Bill understands why I'm so frustrated with you." *How could he? And now he asks if I trust him?*

Her betrayal memory burns like hot coals. She looks at Bill, sitting, leaning back in his chair, always leaning back waiting. *Waiting for an answer, like I'm having a session in his office. Why does he have to be so much like a counselor?*

Wrinkles cross Bill's face.

I've got to tell him something. If I tell him why I can't trust him … The prospect of Bill leaving worries Jill. He's been easy to share personal concerns with. That didn't happen much with Joseph.

Her decision to leave Bill's skeleton in the closet is cut short by Bill's earlier words: "What's important is that Daniel can see that you're trying, that you want to fix things up."

If I tell Bill that I know that he sided with Joseph about leaving me, will he see that I'm trying to fix things, or will it tell him I'm dragging up old wounds, wounds that will separate us? Will he apologize, like I'm supposed to do with Daniel? Jill looks at Bill, trying to predict his response. *If he does apologize, will I feel like I can trust him?*

Answers evade her. Jill begins to suspect that Bill is becoming impatient even though he hasn't moved. His patience irritates her. *If he'd only do something, say something, I could react to that.* She looks down, avoiding Bill's searching eyes. *Do I really care that he took Joseph's side?*

The once-buried grievance causes her to boil. She realizes that if Daniel has issues with her like she has with Bill, then she should know about it.

Taking a deep breath, she looks up and pokes the memory of Bill's disloyalty. "How can you ask me to trust you? You betrayed me." She's surprised at the pain that instantly blankets Bill's face. It takes a couple of seconds before he can speak.

"Whoa! Where is this coming from?" Bill sits up in his chair as he tries to figure out what has given rise to this attack.

"You said you understood why Joseph wanted to leave me. Don't deny it. Joseph told me. I thought you were *my* friend. Then you sided with Joseph? You betrayed me! Now you want me to trust you, to do something I'm not too keen on?"

Controlling his voice, Bill responds, "You're right. I did tell Joseph that I understood *his frustration*. Joseph agreed to buy a house for you that he felt he couldn't afford. To make it work, he put in hours of overtime. Then you criticized him for not spending enough time at home. *That* I said I understood. Not that he leave you. He claimed you were incapable of being loving. I said I thought you were a loving person. I still think so."

"You didn't encourage him to leave me?"

"No. Remember, I tried to bring the two of you together to work out your differences." He pauses. "As for you not being comfortable talking to Daniel, then don't do it. If you have a better solution, go with that. Or if you think you can comfortably continue with the way things are now, then do so."

Jill sits, digesting Bill's response. Her outburst leaves Bill feeling uncomfortable. Using the downing of his second cup of tea, he excuses himself and goes to the washroom. When he comes out, he says it's time to leave. "I'll call when I get back, okay?"

Bill's departure catches her off guard. "*Get back*" triggers her memory. Bill is leaving for a conference. *Really, is he going because I blamed him for taking Joseph's side? "I'll call" We'll continue to see each other.*

"Okay?" repeats Bill.

Jill agrees and waves as he walks to the door.

The next day, Jill tries to reach Julie. It takes several attempts. Her niece is excited about her trip. She monopolizes the early part of the conversation by talking about all the arrangements and packing she's doing for her trip to Ontario. When Jill asks about getting together before she leaves, Julie squeezes her in Wednesday morning. She asks Jill to come to her place.

When Jill arrives at Julie's for their tea break, she finds Julie has streaked her short blonde hair. *Auburn. Nice.* Julie's excitement remains unabated. Her draft itinerary includes visiting her parents and Josey as well as helping Scott's parents pack and move. Jill compliments Julie on her organization.

"Wonderful! Maybe it will also make sense to Scott when I tell him this afternoon."

The conversation turns to Jill's reason for coming over. To Jill's surprise, Julie agrees with asking for Daniel's forgiveness. She's certain he'll grant it.

"You really think so?"

"I do." Julie's confidence fails to encourage Jill. "Wait a minute," says Julie, jumping out of her chair. "If he doesn't, I'll show you what you need to give him." She rushes to a bookshelf in the living room. After she pokes through several books, a triumphant, "Got it!" rings out.

As Julie approaches the table, she says, "You're still his mother. It's never too late to teach your son something." Julie shows her the cover of a book that she and some of the ladies in the church reviewed last year.

The title is *Forgiveness.* Flipping through the pages, she finds a highlighted section. "See," she says, pointing to a quote from Matthew 5:21–25. Then she draws Jill's attention to a couple of verses she sees as key.

> But I tell you, that anyone who is angry with his brother will be subject to judgment

"Think *mother* instead of brother here," interjects Julie. "And this too." She points to another verse.

> Therefore, if you are offering your gift at the altar and there remember that your brother has something against you, leave your gift there in front of the altar. First go and be reconciled to your brother, then come and offer your gift.

"If Daniel doesn't forgive you, how can he continue to go to church?"
"I guess I should have joined you last year for these sessions. May I borrow this book?"

"Definitely. And when I come back, I'll look forward to hearing how well your talk with Daniel works out."

Jill's nod lacks enthusiasm. She hasn't told Julie that her part is identifying what she thinks she has done to offend Daniel. As far as Jill is concerned, she isn't like her parents. She hasn't done anything wrong.

"Cheer up. It'll work out. I'll pray for you."

"Thanks." Jill forces a smile. She realizes the first passage Julie showed her applies as much to her as it does to Daniel. She knows he harbors a deep hostility toward her. She wishes she could remember what caused it.

The week that Bill is away drags for Jill. When she's free of her daily routine, she dwells on Bill's challenge—what caused Daniel's hostility? Nothing comes to mind, but Bill's suggestion continues to haunt her. She wonders what Daniel told Bill or what Joseph told Bill. *I'll bet he knows how I've failed my son.*

I've failed. The idea hangs on her. Turning from how she has disappointed Daniel, she considers Bill's feelings. *I didn't acknowledge his explanation about understanding Joseph's position. He may think I'm still angry with him.*

Reading Julie's Matthew passage, Jill remembers that she told Bill she was uncomfortable asking for Daniel's forgiveness. That statement embarrasses her. She wishes she could delete the comment like she does a sentence on the computer.

A week passes. Jill listens anxiously for the phone to ring. Bill's last words, "I'll call you when I get back," offer hope. As the afternoon slips by and Bill hasn't called, she realizes that she is assuming that Bill will call her the first day he is back. The possibility that he might call the next day or even next week nudges her to call Bill. She decides she'll phone after supper, after the dishes are done. She needs to hear his voice, to hear that there's no sense of being hurt by her implying he chose Joseph over her.

While preparing supper, she evaluates her relationship with Bill and determines a missing element. She plans how to remedy it. Then the phone rings. Like a schoolgirl, Jill races to answer it. She forces herself to relax. It's Bill. The news that the conference went smoothly and his friend is well takes second place. Jill's relieved to hear Bill talk. She detects no hint of duty or responsibility for having to call her. *We're still friends.*

"So we're still on for Sunday dinner?" asks Bill.

Yes! thinks Jill. It's the question she has been waiting for.

"We've always eaten at my place, or we've gone out for supper," says Jill. "How about we eat at your place this time?"

"No problem. I might have an interesting surprise for you too."

His acceptance comes so quickly it surprises Jill. She looks forward to seeing his place. *Your house will tell me a lot about you.*

Bill's instructions bring Jill to a property screened by a thick stretch of mature birch trees. The landmark, a black chain-link fence between the road and the trees, assures Jill she has found the right place. After turning into the driveway, she is greeted by a redbrick ranch-style house. As she drives up the long, paved driveway, the smell of fresh-cut lawn reminds her of the farm. She judges his place to be twice the size of Josey's Brampton property.

At Jill's request, Bill tours her through his five-bedroom house. She walks past his closed study door, and she asks if she can take a peek inside. He shrugs. She quickly opens the door. Only a container filled with ballpoint pens and a navy plastic pouch sits on the desk. Large white lettering on the navy pouch catches her eye—Chamber of Commerce, Saskatoon. She guesses that's where Bill's conference took place. In front of the desk, a wall-mounted bookshelf displays neatly arranged books. A quick scan tells Jill they mostly deal with people management and psychology. She turns to leave, in response to Bill's call, "You coming?" Seven framed awards, hanging on the inside wall, momentarily stop her. With no time to read them, she notes a faint Caterpillar Company logo on three of the awards' backgrounds. The bold black italics "***Outstanding***" impresses her. Jill catches up to Bill in the family room. The brick fireplace reminds Jill of what she and Joseph shared on the farm.

Outside on the back patio, Bill stands in the shade of a forty-foot pine tree. Before him is a screened firebox with wood and kindling waiting for the match. To the side, a white patio table and two chairs await them. Two glasses and a bottle of wine sit on the table.

"Do you want a quick look at where I do my gardening, or would you rather relax by the fire with a glass of wine?"

"I think the wine will keep for five or ten minutes," says Jill. She walks past Bill to examine his perennial garden bordering the west side of the patio. The many roses she sees remind her of Josey's flower bed by the patio. Sweet peas clinging to a chain-link fence in a one-foot raised planter draw her to them to see if they have a fragrance left. A few late blossoms reward her. She fingers the dry pods packed with seeds. Together, they stroll out to Bill's small vegetable garden. Except for some carrots and kale, the rest has been tilled. Jill recognizes stands of poplar and maples in the distance. She admires two Russian olive trees and two old oaks. Their height fascinates her. She guesses they've been here for forty, fifty, maybe even sixty years.

When they return to the patio, Bill sets a match to the wood in his firebox. The dry kindling catches quickly. As he sits at the table with Jill, he says, "I remember how much you said you like watching a fire and that you like a glass of wine."

"The wine's usually for special occasions."

"And this is a special occasion. This is the first time that you've come to my place. What do you think of it?" He pours wine into Jill's glass and then his own.

"Unbelievable! Kind of a large place for you, your wife, and one son."

"Actually, we didn't get it until after Mark went to Saudi Arabia. Donna inherited it from her mother. I thought it was too much for us too. When I suggested we sell it, she refused. She wanted to move in. Her childhood memories comforted her, especially after she was sick."

Jill would like to know more about Mark, but she focuses on Bill. "Now your memories of her comfort you and root you here."

Bill smells his wine. "My sanctuary, but I am trying to move on."

"And you have let me come to this special place. Thank you. I'm honored."

Their glasses clink.

Bill takes a deep breath and with new energy says, "Enough about me. How about you? Tell me how you did on discovering what has poisoned Daniel's attitude toward you."

"Boy! Do you change topics fast!"

"And you're good at trying to evade answers. I'm assuming you still want to make amends with him."

"Yes."

"So did you come up with anything?"

"Nothing that I think is really a cause. My guess is Daniel's frustration grew sometime after I had Amber. I thought maybe he was jealous of the attention I paid to Amber. You know, a new baby requires a lot of care."

"And as Amber grew older?"

"Later, I became Amber's kindergarten teacher and then her schoolteacher. That drew us even closer. I wanted to be Daniel's home schoolteacher too. That way, I'd be treating both children equally. He wouldn't think I was favoring Amber."

"That didn't happen?"

"No. Daniel didn't seem to be interested. Joseph favored Daniel continuing with the church school too. I thought that all Daniel needed to see is that homeschooling could work well. Amber showed she was happy with it. When I tried to get Daniel to let me teach him at home a year later, Joseph said no. He was very adamant, so I dropped it."

"Didn't Joseph give any indication why he thought Daniel wanted to remain in the church school?"

"He said Daniel wanted to stay with his friends."

"Friends are important."

"So is family."

"How were Daniel's grades?"

"Honors …" She pauses. "All the time." Jill takes a sip of her wine and studies Bill's thoughtful expression. "Think of something?"

"Could it be that Daniel earned his high marks so you wouldn't have a reason to transfer him from the church school?"

"I never thought of that."

"A fear of you taking him away from his friends might cause a deep-seated anger. From that base, it could spread to other actions that he didn't like you taking."

"Do you think that's why he's so angry with me?"

"I don't know. I'm exploring possibilities. What's more important is whether you think that is a possibility. What do you think?"

Jill recalls some of the women in the Orthodox Community Church labeling her as being selfish because she wanted to have her children at home with her. *If Daniel overheard those conversations, he too might think I was selfish. That would anger him.*

"I don't know. That could be the reason. Then it might not be. What do I do?"

"Do you really want to be on good terms with your son?"

"Yes."

"Then, if you think your attempts to homeschool him are the basis for the tension between the two of you, apologize to him. Ask him to forgive you. Explain that you didn't realize at the time how important it was for him to be with his friends."

"And what if that's not the real reason?"

"It doesn't matter. You're showing him you want to improve the family atmosphere. If you're wrong, let him identify what he thinks is the problem. At least you're starting the healing process."

"Do you think that is why Daniel is so hostile toward me?" Jill suspects Bill knows something that he's not telling her.

"What I think doesn't matter. What counts is what you think is the root of your family problem. If you're wrong, don't worry about it. He'll see that you're attempting to improve things. The ball will then be in his court."

Bill leans back in his chair while Jill thinks about different approaches that she could use in talking to Daniel. Not to appear impatient, Bill puts a few sticks of poplar into his burning bin and pokes the coals. When he looks back, he sees her shaking her head.

"Something wrong?"

"I don't think I can do it," she confesses. "Whatever I come up with sounds like I'm making excuses. That'll never work."

"The fact that you can recognize what doesn't work proves you will come up with the right words. And if you don't, don't worry. No one is perfect. You can do it. I'm sure of it. Trust me."

"I don't know."

"Jill, you really have to work on that trust. Believe me when I say I know you can do it."

"But I don't want to blow it."

"Do you want help?"

"You can't tell me what to say. It has to come from me."

"You're right, but I know how I can help you come up with the right words."

"How?"

"Pray."

"Pray?"

"Yes. Pray. Let's ask God to lead you in your talk with Daniel."

"I don't know."

"You sound like Moses when he said to the Lord that he didn't have the ability to speak to pharaoh. Remember, God gave him the ability he needed."

"That's in the Bible. That's a long time ago."

"You don't think it happens today?"

"Not to my knowledge. I've never heard anyone claim that God inspired them to say anything of value."

"Then hear it now. Many times in talking with clients at the Wellness Center and even when I was the personnel manager, I've said things I never thought of. Sometimes I said things in ways I wouldn't have imagined. I've given thanks to the Lord for opening my eyes, or rather opening my mouth at the right time, and saying the right things. Believe me, it pays to ask for the Lord's guidance in uncertain times."

Bill speaks with such confidence that Jill refrains from challenging him. Her doubts continue to plague her to the point of considering giving up on the idea of talking to Daniel.

Jill's continuing silence prompts Bill to ask, "Would you like me to pray with you, to ask for the Lord's leading on this healing venture?"

Jill nods.

Bill draws his chair close to Jill. He takes her hands in his, and they bow their heads.

"Dear Father in heaven, thank you for listening to your children, particularly in their times of need. Today, Jill and I come to you to ask you for your blessing as she attempts to bring about reconciliation between Daniel and herself. You know the fears that hold Jill back. Make them disappear in the confidence that she will know that you will be with her. Give her a compassionate ear and the words that she needs to initiate this healing. Give her the insight to see and know that you are with her, helping her so she can turn to you more often in the future. We ask for these blessings in the name of Jesus Christ. Amen."

"Thank you. Now can we change topics?" Jill pulls her hands back.

The pleading look in Jill's eyes causes Bill to laugh. "Certainly. What would you like to talk about?"

"Why you went to Saskatoon?"

"Saskatoon?"

"I saw the label on the pouch in your study." Jill holds her glass out for more wine.

"To speak at a conference. I told you that."

"What's so new about your message that the chamber of commerce wants you to address their members?"

"I'm not sure what I have to say is so new as it is to reaffirm what they already know. I provided a few studies to give them confidence that my claims are based on scientific evidence as well as practical experience."

With Jill's encouragement, Bill describes the work he did as a personnel manager with his former employer. The key principal of his presentation was personnel managers need to be out of their office connecting with people in the company. By talking to them about their home life and work, businessmen and women demonstrate an interest in their workers' welfare. Involving the company in solving workers' problems, like addictions, earns the staff's goodwill. At times, it means the company's decision makers participate in the workers' social functions. The success reported by his company proves his ideas work.

"I think employers really appreciated the effect of diminishing interests in unions." Bill chuckles with the last conclusion.

"While you were in Saskatchewan, you visited a friend."

"Whenever one can incorporate a little pleasure with a business trip, it's a bonus."

"That friend was Joseph, wasn't it?"

"What gives you that idea?"

"I helped Amber move. I noticed that the painting that she did recently isn't at the apartment. I didn't see it at Mary's place either. I figure she gave it to you to take to Joseph."

"I told Amber seeing her father wasn't out of my way. She was so happy."

"How is he doing?"

"At the moment, struggling. Economically," he adds. "I think that should change soon. I put him in touch with a businessman I met at the conference. The guy has a construction project, so I recommended Joseph. Joseph will do a good job, and word will get around. More jobs will eventually come to him."

"That must have made his day."

"Yes. He was so pleased that he invited me to his place. As a matter of fact, because of that visit, I'm in a good position to offer a special meal, one that he showed me how to make."

"Really! And what may I ask is it?"

"We made pierogis together. He said you and the girls used to help him make it. Then you served ham with it. He said you always enjoyed that meal, so I thought I would surprise you with it tonight."

"You shouldn't have. That's a lot of work."

"Oh, I didn't make it today. Joseph and I made a hundred when I was there. We froze what we didn't eat. Some of those came home with me. That's what we're eating tonight."

"You shouldn't have. That was for you."

"I thought who better to share them with?"

"That's just like you! Always out to impress."

"Thanks."

"You know you don't have to earn someone's approval. You're a very good man."

"You say that because you know me now."

"I had that impression of you at the conference. And I just met you."

"You did?"

"Yes. What I'm puzzled about is why you bother with me. And don't say I am a good person."

"But you are."

"I'm not. That's why I'm divorced now. I drove a good man away. Why bother with someone like me?"

"Like I said. At the conference, you accepted me as I was even though I expressed my misgivings about not being with Donna in the hospital. I felt like I was abandoning her when she needed me most. I felt like a total jerk. But you were there for me when I needed somebody. I won't forget that. So when I got the call to pick up your children, I thought it was my time to return a favor."

"But then you continued to see me in the hospital."

"I thought you still needed me."

"But not that you still owed me. Picking up my children would have been more than enough. Even so, you wouldn't have expected me to sue you for not balancing the books."

"I didn't want to abandon you like I did Donna."

"Then there's the help you gave Amber. And after I came home from the hospital. You didn't have to keep in touch with me. I don't mean to sound ungrateful, but it almost seems like you were trying to earn my approval, like you did something before to offend me."

"No. No. It's nothing like that."

"Then what?"

Bill looks at the ground. "I don't really want to say. I'm afraid you won't think much of me. Then I'll lose you."

Jill moves her chair even closer to Bill's. She reaches over and picks up his hand. "Bill, I like you. I like you very much. You can tell me anything."

Bill slowly looks up. Worry shadows his face.

"I want to see our relationship grow." She pauses to assess Bill's reaction. When he doesn't try to pull away, she continues, "But you have to let me into your life. You have to trust me." Jill smiles as she echoes the words Bill often uses on her.

"I don't know. I think you won't like what you hear." His voice is very low.

"And you say I have trust issues."

Bill smiles. Still in a barely audible tone, he asks, "Promise you'll forgive me if I sound out of line?"

With her nod, he begins, "About a week before Donna died, in rationed words, she asked me for a favor. From the time it took to summon enough strength to speak, I knew it had to be important. I still remember her words—*Favor? Promise?* I agreed. It didn't matter what she would ask, I knew I would agree."

Tears fill Bill's eyes. He looks down and starts crying. Jill slides her chair beside Bill's and holds him in her arms. Before continuing, he apologizes.

"What was her favor?"

Looking at Jill and using his fingers, he wipes water from his eyes. "She said when she was gone, I should find another woman to look after me." He wipes fresh tears away. "She led in a prayer. She asked God to help me find someone. When she finished, she fell asleep. That was the second-to-last time she spoke. Two days later, she whispered, '*I love you.*'"

Bill starts crying. Jill holds him until he stops. When he looks up again, he says, "I didn't tell her I couldn't honor my promise. I didn't want to take a chance on facing another separation from someone I loved. Mark flew down from Saudi Arabia. He had a month off. We supported each other. Then he flew back. For a while, he'd phone. It ended after a month.

"I tried to keep myself busy by tending the yard and going to church. By fall, I knew I needed some other activity to take my mind off Donna. I didn't want to replace Donna. Preparing meals at the Wellness Center helped. It filled the day, especially in the winter. Come spring, I returned to serving the drop-ins who came in the afternoon. Listening to their concerns and suggesting alternate solutions came naturally to me.

"Then one afternoon, as I was driving to the Wellness Center, I received your call. I canceled my time at the center and picked up your children. Talking to them felt so good. A forgotten piece of my life came back to me. When Julie asked me for help, I couldn't resist. I still questioned my involvement. I felt like I was a vulture swooping in where I wasn't really wanted. Opportunities to help continued. Gradually, I became more involved with Julie and later Amber."

"I'm glad you did," says Jill.

"Still, without your input, I felt out of place. I was slipping into your family's life without your permission. I looked for a sign that said I should back away. My conversations with Julie and Rebecca and Thomas and later with Mary showed me I should continue. And visiting you in the hospital—it seemed my being with Donna in the hospital prepared me for visiting you. It was like God had trained me for that service. I found myself praying for your recovery, looking forward to us talking again, like we did in Chicago. Then when you came to, I felt like my prayers were answered. Because you seemed to enjoy our conversations in the hospital and in the garden, I kept returning."

"I did enjoy them," says Jill.

"Then you were gone. I missed you. I told myself I didn't have any place in your family. It was your family, not mine. I thanked God for the time we shared together and accepted that as the blessing. My consolation was that I found that it was possible for me to enjoy the company of another woman.

"Your phone call inviting me to come for Sunday dinner renewed my hope. I thought we might be able to spend some time together again. The more we met, the more I looked forward to meeting again. At the same time, I worried that I wasn't being completely honest with you. Somehow, you'd find out and be angry with me."

"So you aren't shopping around for another wife?"

"Just your company in any way I can have it."

"Good. I like things as they are," says Jill, feeling relieved. "What do you say we try that supper you and Joseph cooked up?"

Jill asks Bill how well he remembers how to make the pierogis. In response to his hesitant answer, Jill points out that practice is the best way to make sure one remembers what to do. Since practice should take place relatively soon after the lesson, she recommends they schedule the following Saturday to make more pierogis.

Bill's refresher lesson starts early in the afternoon. He plans to make one hundred, knowing that Matthew and Sarah would enjoy them too. He suggests serving them for Sunday's supper as compensation for them having to make their own spaghetti supper Saturday.

After Jill and Bill finish their meal and wash the pots, bowls, and dishes, Jill declares that Bill has passed. "All the pierogis sealed. I think you've got the hang of it."

Taking a bottle of wine and two glasses, Bill suggests they celebrate. He heads to the fireplace in the family room and lights the fire. In the warmth of the fire and the effects of a glass of wine, he asks about her children. He learns that Amber finds campus life lonely. She appreciates Mary and Ed's company. Sarah's English class has challenged her to think about a future career—food nutritionist or alternative medicine. After she relates Matthew's disappointment over his volleyball game loss, she asks Bill if he's heard from his son.

Ignoring her question, he asks, "Aren't you missing someone?"

Jill thinks for a moment. "You mean Daniel?"

"Right."

"You're wondering if I tried to call him yet?"

"Yes."

"No, I haven't, because I don't know what I'm going to say."

"Have you been praying about it?"

"No, I haven't."

"I've been praying for you."

Jill says nothing. Her blank look prompts him to continue.

"Maybe that's why you don't feel comfortable in calling Daniel."

Jill gives a slight shrug and continues looking at Bill with a blank expression.

Bill searches for a way to engage Jill. "Tell me, how would you like to go next Saturday for a visit to Mary and Ed's?"

"Really? Yes!"

Bill smiles. "And how would you like it if that request came to you via Julie?"

"Why would you do that? You can ask me directly."

"Exactly. You might wonder why I would go through someone else if I was really serious about going to Edmonton."

Jill is already guessing where Bill's going with his example, but Bill continues, intent on making sure he is understood.

"That's my point. If you really want to straighten things out between you and Daniel, you would ask your Father in heaven for help. Don't leave it up to me."

"That's not easy for me to do."

Jill looks at the flames leaping about. She needs their energetic distraction. Seeing disappointment or shock in Bill's eyes is not an option.

"I told Joseph about my father. I asked him not to ever yell at me, and he didn't. Only once, he raised his voice. It was only one word. *No.* That was the last time I asked Joseph if Daniel could take homeschooling. I was too afraid to push the issue again. I'm still afraid to bring it up."

The fire's crackling hides the silence that blankets them. Finally, Jill stands up.

"I think it's time I leave. I've shown you I'm a weird woman."

Before she completes half a turn, Bill is on his feet. He catches her and turns her back to him.

"Look at me."

She shakes her head.

"Please."

"Why?" She continues looking down.

"I want you to see how important you are to me."

Jill slowly raises her head and sees a concerned focus.

"Do my questions about Daniel make you uncomfortable?" His voice is soft as if talking to a little child.

"Most of the time, no." She pauses before she adds, "But now I am. You must think I'm a willful, disobedient, weak, stupid woman."

"More like a frightened woman and with good reason. I think you can still fix things. There may be a way."

Jill studies Bill's thoughtful face. She feels he's taking a long time to let her in on his supposed saving strategy.

"Remember I told you that God answers my prayers? He carries me through my trials?"

"Yes."

"Can you rely on my confidence that he'll bless you in your effort to make things right with Daniel?"

After a brief pause, Jill nods.

"Good. Then can I ask you for a tiny favor?"

Jill nods again, not trusting her voice.

"Will you sit with me and watch the fire go out? That way, I won't worry later that I scared you off by being so outspoken."

Jill smiles and nods.

"Maybe you might want to throw on a few more pieces of wood so I can stay a little longer."

"Great idea."

He does Jill's bidding before he sits down next to her. He draws her close, knowing she'll be welcoming him tomorrow for supper with her children.

Jill's desire to meet with Daniel grows stronger over the next few days. She calls Bill.

"Bill, I need your help."

"What would you like?"

"For you to be with me when I meet with Daniel? I don't need you to say anything, just be there."

"Like moral support?"

"Kind of, yes."

"No problem. When and where?"

"Originally, I thought of asking Daniel to come over here at the end of his day on Saturday. Sarah's at work, but sometimes Matthew brings his friends over to play games."

"And you don't want any distractions."

"Right. Which is why I didn't want to meet him at work or at his home."

"Why not meet at my place? That way, there'll only be the three of us."

"Thanks. I was hoping you'd say that."

"Would you like me to phone him and ask him over? I could say I have a delicate matter I want him to consider."

"Well, that's not exactly true."

"Actually it is. At the celebration party at Mary's, Eve asked me if I could help her with Daniel's attitude toward you. I told her I would try. You being here shows I'm working on it."

"Do you think he'll come?"

"Hopefully he doesn't have anything else planned. If there is a problem, I'll call you."

The next three days, Jill waits, expecting Bill to say Daniel canceled. The call doesn't come. Following Bill's advice, each evening before she goes to bed, she prays to God, asking for his guidance and strength. As the day nears when she is to meet with Daniel, she worries. She still has no idea what she is going to say to her son, how she is even going to start. Bill's words come back to comfort her. "God will provide you with what you need when you need it. Have faith that he'll be there for you."

The evening before she is to meet with Daniel, she debates baking a pan of cheese buns. Daniel always loved them. He used to gobble the whole pan in an evening if she didn't call for some restraint. Once she made double the recipe. Before she caught him, he'd eaten twice his normal helping. *Can't do it*, decides Jill. *It will be a distraction*. Not wanting to deny him a treat, she plans to bake a couple of pans of buns for his birthday.

As Jill drives up to Bill's house, her attention is on the first thing she is going to say to Daniel. She wants to state what is obvious—there's a noticeable tension between them. At first, she thinks it's a useless thing to say. It's obvious, but she concludes that is not what will be on Daniel's mind when he comes over. "Make no assumptions," she tells herself.

Bill greets her as she steps out of her Malibu. "Ready?"

"No, but I'm here. I sure hope everything works out."

"It will. Don't worry. I have confidence in you."

"You know Daniel's birthday is in three weeks. If this goes well, I hope he'll invite us to come."

"Us?"

"Yes. You will come with me, won't you?"

"Since you're asking, sure I will." When they approach the door, Bill stops Jill. "Want to walk a little of that nervous energy off? We can stroll to the far end of the yard and back."

Jill agrees. They work their way to the end of his property line. On their return, Bill says, "You know when I find walking around the yard especially rewarding?" Without waiting for Jill to respond, he continues,

"Before some big event, like the Saskatoon conference. The day before I flew out, I spent an hour wandering around. I find looking at nature comforting. Everything here seems to work out perfectly. To me, it's like nature's testimony that God is in control. From that, I take it I won't make a fool of myself."

"I never thought of it that way," says Jill. "But it is reassuring."

Seeing that they have at least twenty minutes before Daniel arrives, Bill asks Jill to look at some area rugs on the computer. He's considering replacing the one that's in the family room. He hopes the diversion will ease Jill's tension. The forty-minute distraction works. Jill doesn't realize that Daniel is late. The closing of his truck door reminds her of the main reason she is there.

Bill hurries out and escorts Daniel to the kitchen. When they enter, Jill comes from the family room and joins them.

"I thought that was Mom's car. What's this all about?" Daniel looks at Bill for an explanation.

Jill looks at him, expecting him to explode. He's her height but trim and muscular like his father. She focuses on his soiled company cap, a small tear on the side of his loose, no-longer-white T-shirt; black paint-stained jeans; and ragged runners.

"Let's sit down first." Bill points to the table and then models his instructions. Jill does the same. As Bill hopes, Daniel follows their lead.

"I told you I had a delicate matter for you to consider. I thought it best if I invite a person who has more detailed knowledge about it to talk to you." He points to Jill.

Be short and to the point, Jill tells herself. *Admit I was wrong and ask him to forgive me.*

"Daniel, there's a noticeable tension between us. Eve's noticed it. Bill's noticed it. I'm sure you're aware of it. I know I'm aware of it. And it's starting to create problems." Jill expects the next words to come out of her mouth to be, *and I want it stopped.* "I really want to see if we can put a stop to this." Jill appreciates her improved phrasing. "I've been trying to figure out what I've done to anger you. Now, I could be completely wrong about this, but I suspect your anger has been simmering for a long time. I'm wondering if it has anything, anything at all, to do with my desire to have you take homeschooling when you were little."

Jill notices surprise on Daniel's face.

"At the time, I wanted you to be home with Amber and me so we could be a close family. My mistake was not thinking about what you wanted. Your father had to straighten me out." She pauses. The first sentence is all she intended to say. "More than once. I want to apologize for thinking only of what I wanted. I'm sure you can probably think of more examples like that, but I want to tell you I plan to be more careful. Do you think you can even begin to forgive me?"

"You're right. I've been seeing you as selfish for a long time. I often wanted to tell you that to your face, but Dad wouldn't let me. You say you're changing. I'll have to learn to start seeing that. I don't know how well I will do. My instinctive reaction is to suspect you don't care about anyone except yourself. It's become a habit. I can tell you that I'll work on it, but I may not always see it."

"Me too, Daniel. I'll work on taking your feelings into consideration. My habit won't be any easier to break."

"As for forgiving you, I can say I will start. Forgiving you means I can accept you had good reasons for your actions. I don't know what they are. And I don't want to know, at least not right now. I'm afraid I may take them as excuses. All I can say is that for now, I will assume you had good reasons. Maybe, in time, I will be ready to hear and understand them. Is that fair?"

"Yes, Daniel. A start is all I ask." Jill has an overwhelming urge to rush over and hug Daniel, but she sees no sign of him being willing to accept it. His squirming suggests uneasiness.

"I'm sure you must realize this all comes as a shock to me. My desire to leave now means I need time to work this development out." He glances at Bill and then again at his mother.

"Certainly," says Bill.

Jill echoes his response.

Daniel says his goodbyes and leaves without looking back. When Jill hears his truck drive off, she says, "Sounds hopeful, don't you think?"

Bill agrees.

"But I get the impression he seems a little disappointed. Maybe he doesn't want to change his impression of me?" Jill looks at Bill.

"He's grown comfortable in thinking of you in one particular way. He thinks he knows what to expect. That makes it easy, if not comfortable. The good news is he's aware that he's called to change. But change is never easy. Think of the stories you've heard about people trying to quit smoking. Some try several times. Those failures do nothing to boost their ego. That's what he's facing."

Jill thinks of some of the men at the Orthodox Community Church, their smoking in her presence, their not caring. *Sure, some might smoke outside, but the cigarette stench sticks to their clothes.* The possibility that they're trying and failing reduces her antagonism.

The first effect of Jill's talk with Daniel comes in a few days. Eve phones and invites Jill and the rest of the family to Daniel's birthday party. Jill asks if Bill can come with her. Eve happily agrees.

The invitation for Bill to come to Daniel's birthday party sparks an invitation from Bill. He asks Jill and the rest of the family to join him in visiting Thomas and Rebecca. He knows that that is something the Croschuks have been looking forward to for some time. Since Jill hadn't taken his hint that she should visit them earlier, he thinks she might come with him. Jill accepts. The success of that visit leads to Jill joining him every second Friday.

A new routine for Saturday afternoons develops. Jill spends her afternoons with Bill. The change began when they started car shopping. Cooking together followed. The conversation with Daniel became a natural progression. Bill's invitation to help him shop for a new area rug online changes to going to the businesses. One Saturday, Bill takes her to the Oden restaurant in the Norseman for her birthday. Another Saturday, at Amber's suggestion, they visit Mary and Ed and go to see Candy Cane Lane in Edmonton.

CHRISTMAS BRINGS FAMILIES TOGETHER

LAST YEAR FOR CHRISTMAS, Bill didn't decorate his house or set up a Christmas tree. The loss of his wife eight months earlier and the fact that Mark, his son, was unable to get time off from work to fly down for the holiday dampened his spirit. Jill too confessed to a lack of Christmas spirit last year. Because of her divorce, the children had initiated the season's celebrations. While they had a tree, there was no Christmas Eve dinner, no turkey the next day.

Prompted by Jill's confession of her children's disappointment about the last Christmas, Bill proposes that his house be used for the season's celebrations. He suggests that they get together so they can prepare some of the Christmas Eve dishes. Excited by her quick acceptance, Bill offers to phone Daniel to see if his family will join them for Christmas dinner at his place. Jill doesn't expect Daniel to accept, but she agrees to the call. Daniel accepts.

A week before Christmas Day, Bill phones Jill. In a casual tone, he requests a change. Can meal preparations start two days earlier? Jill counters with, "How about Saturday?" She explains by the time she comes home from work and makes and eats supper, there wouldn't be much time to cook. "If we don't finish Saturday, I'll have Monday off. I'll be able to help."

Bill's hesitation prompts Jill to ask, "Why the change?"

"My son just phoned. He's coming to spend Christmas and New Year's with me. He flies in from Saudi Arabia on the twenty-second." Bill explains the late notice is because Mark's company didn't authorize his holidays even though they had it a month ago. Mark waited until he received his pay yesterday. Then he showed his boss the one-way ticket to go home to visit his father. He told them if they wanted to accept his absence as a month's holidays, they could buy him a return ticket.

"They agreed," says Bill, excited. "I hope you'll like him."

"We did it!" says Jill as she sets the platter of leftover turkey on the counter.

Bill puts the bowl of mashed potatoes and a half-empty cranberry sauce container on the counter. "But we wouldn't have had the turkey ready if you and your children hadn't come here before church. How in the world did you get your children to get up so early?"

"I told the kids we could open the presents before we went to church, but I had to get the turkey in the oven first. So we ate a quick breakfast, packed up our presents, and rushed here."

Jill and Bill turn around to collect the dirty dinner dishes from the table.

"Okay, you two," says Eve. She approaches them with a stack of plates. "To the family room. Bill, you aren't going to spend another minute cleaning up when your son is in the next room. Go and enjoy his company. We'll take care of everything here."

"Eve, you don't need to do that," says Jill.

"You're right. So call it my Christmas present to Bill." She marches past Bill and sets her load down. A gentle shove starts Bill on his way.

"Go, Mom," says Amber as she brings the glasses from the table.

"Yes," echoes Sarah. She too carries a tray of cups.

Jill follows their instructions. They enter the family room to find Matthew sitting next to Daniel on the chesterfield. Daniel is holding Shawn. His three girls are playing on the floor near him. They brought the toys they received that morning.

Daniel looks to Mark. "So what exactly is it that you do?" asks Daniel as he bounces his son on his knee.

Mark is tall, clean-shaven, and neatly dressed like his father, but he has no receding hairline. The physical demands of his job leave him in excellent shape. *Like Daniel*, thinks Jill. *Wonder why no girl's snagged him yet.*

"Just a minute," says Jill. She grabs a chair. "I want to hear this too."

Bill takes another chair and sits by Jill.

Grinning, Mark begins, "You could say I'm a floater. Wherever the company needs me, that's where I go—set up, repairs, welding, drilling, even security. Many of our workers are young. Keeping them isn't easy. Lately, as in the last four years, I've been training, actually mentoring would be more like it."

"What's the difference?" asks Daniel as he shifts Shawn to his other knee.

"Training is skill building. That's relatively easy. Mentoring is working with new employees. I not only teach them skills, but I make a point of getting to know them and their families, help them see how the company helps them live a good life."

"Sounds like that's beyond your job description. Probably takes up a lot more time too."

"You're right, Daniel. That's exactly what my supervisor said too when he found out what I was up to. The thing is, the people who work with me have stayed with the company. They don't quit."

"How come?"

"Because when I learn what's important to their family life, I always link the family goals with the company's goals and their paychecks. Frequently, I know the wife and the children. I praise the father in their presence and talk to them about their family goals. Thanks to what I learn from the wife and the children, I'm able to motivate the men to work longer hours or tackle assignments they'd rather not."

"Did your job description change?" Daniel notices Shawn yawning. He cradles him in his arms, hoping he'll drift off.

"The title and description. They're still trainers. There is no mentor designation. Because of the extra hours I put in outside of company time, they would have to pay me much higher. It's probably why they resist acknowledging my recommended position. Imagine being paid to go out to supper with fellow employees or join them at some sports event. I don't get time and a half, but I am paid for the visits I make. I meet some very wonderful people and enjoy some excellent meals. I have two guys in the company who are working with me to become mentors."

"Sounds like you love your job," observes Jill.

"I do, and to tell you the truth, the pay is very good."

"Tell us more about the ordinary life." Matthew's change of topic causes Bill to stand up.

"Why don't I bring your album," volunteers Bill.

"Good idea."

When Bill returns with Mark's three-inch-thick photo album, he sees Mark sitting at the feet of Daniel and Matthew. Jill takes Mark's place on the couch to see the pictures. Bill sits back, content to hear Mark. He's seen the album and heard the stories the first night Mark came to his place.

When Eve and her two helpers appear in the family room, they catch the tail end of Mark's description of life in Saudi Arabia. They also see Shannon curled up in Jill's arms. Sharon is sitting on the armrest on the far side of Daniel, and Shelly is squeezed in between Daniel and Matthew.

"Cozy group," says Eve as she admires the family setting. Amber notices the low fire and adds three more poplar logs. "I hope they haven't been wearing you out?" Eve glances at her watch.

"Oh no," responds Bill. "Mark enjoys being the star of the night."

"Dad's right. When I visit the families of the guys I'm mentoring, I'm usually in observing mode. It's great to be the center of attention. It's been a wonderful time."

"I'm glad to hear that," says Jill. "I loved hearing your stories."

"Too bad you're here for such a short time," says Eve.

"You're right," says Mark. "Maybe we can get together again soon. What do you guys do for New Year's Eve?"

A hope springs out of Amber. "Last year, nothing, but we used to play games until midnight. Then we'd have a pizza and some wine."

"Games?" Mark is puzzled.

"Charades, dominos," says Sarah, catching Amber's dream.

"Why don't we do that again this year?" volunteers Daniel. Jill looks at Daniel in surprise.

"We can have it here," offers Bill.

"Great idea," says Mark, excited. "It's been a long time since I've played those games. I look forward to relearning them."

Daniel glances down at Shawn and Shelly, both of whom are sleeping. "Think we can get your parents to babysit?" He looks at his wife.

"I'm sure they can be convinced," answers Eve. "But maybe we should be taking them home now."

Daniel and Eve dress and pack their children into the car. Jill goes outside to see them off. When she returns, she sees her children crowded close to the fire. Mark's nowhere to be seen. Bill is standing back, enjoying the children staring at the leaping flames.

When Bill sees Jill, he tiptoes away from the family room and whispers, "Mark's not feeling well. He's gone to the bathroom. He won't admit it, but I think he overate."

Jill looks at him in surprise.

"Would you like to go out?" He holds his stomach. "Maybe walk off a little of the delicious meal you prepared."

"*We* prepared."

"Let's walk, just up and down the driveway a few times?" Bill looks at her children. "They'll be content to sit there for a while."

The minus five and light breeze makes the anticipated stroll inviting. As they walk away from the house, the bright stars blink from their inky-black drop. Jill remembers the night walks on the farm. No artificial lights to compromise the heavenly contrast. The walk back with the colorful Christmas light display reminds her of how much she enjoyed helping Bill decorate his house.

They start their second walk away from the house. Jill decides to explore possibilities of solving her problem. "I know it's a bit early, that is it's not New Year's Day yet, but do you have any dreams for the next year?"

"Maybe one," says Bill slowly. "At this point, it seems such a reach that I don't place much hope of achieving it. I couldn't have predicted how this year would have turned out, so I'll just be patient and see what happens. What about you?"

"I do have one hope, one I really want to do. But at the same time, I really don't want to do it. Crazy, hey?"

"Conflicted anyway. What is it?"

"Going to Ontario in the summer." Jill chooses her words carefully so her description will sound like her hope is no big deal.

"Because?"

Jill tells him about her grandmother, how loving she was, how Jill ran away from her and wrote her out of her life until Julie reported about Josey on her last visit. Bill asks if guilt for treating her grandmother that way is the reason for Jill's hesitancy in returning.

"It's much worse than that," admits Jill. "I've had some experiences in Oshawa that I don't want to face."

"Would it help if you had someone with you to face them?"

Jill looks at Bill to see if he is serious. "Nice of you to offer, but I did some things back there that I'm not proud of."

"Seems to me I have shared some things in my past that I'm not proud of. Could you tell me about them? If you know how strongly I feel about you, you should know that your past wouldn't bother me."

"I couldn't ask you to go to Oshawa. That's a long way to go. There's nothing there for you."

"Oshawa, that's not too far from the Canadian honeymoon capital, is it?"

"You mean Niagara Falls?"

Bill nods. He puts his arm around Jill's waist and draws her closer.

"I think you're right. I've never been there."

"That's perfect. I haven't either. Maybe we can see it together. Who knows? My impossible dream might not be that impossible."

"Bill, when we are in Oshawa, you might see a real ugly side of me. I don't know if I want you to see that."

Bill notices Jill's tentative acceptance of him coming with her.

"If that's your big problem, maybe it's important that I be there with you to help you deal with it. Can you think of anyone better to come?"

Jill shakes her head. "I'll think about it, if you're sure you're willing."

Bill nods. Wanting to strengthen Jill's resolve to go, he asks her to tell him more about her grandmother. He guesses the more she remembers about her, the more Jill will want to go.

They reach the end of the driveway and return to the house. Jill's stories about her grandmother give Bill a clearer idea of how important Josey is. Upon entering the family room, they see Matthew poking glowing embers. He tosses in the remaining chips from the woodbin.

Amber hears Bill behind her. She turns and says, "We didn't look for more wood. We thought Mom would want to leave soon."

Bill nods his approval.

"Did Mark come back here?" Jill looks around for Bill's son.

"I heard him hurry to the bathroom a while ago. I think he returned to his bedroom," says Matthew as he draws the screen before the fireplace.

"Mind if I go see how he's doing?" asks Jill, looking at Bill.

After Bill nods, she asks her children to pack up their presents and get their clothes. She leaves to see Mark.

Bill picks up the present Amber gave to her mother. When Amber approaches, he asks, "Is this the painting you were talking about the day I came for supper, you know after your mom came home from the hospital?"

"Yes. I think it's like her grandmother's house in Brampton. I tried to catch everything Mom talked about. I designed the balcony using the house we first lived in when we moved into Camrose. That's why the second-floor balcony is divided by square redbrick pillars and edged with a black metal railing."

"And the chimes, is that how she described them?" Bill remembers Jill talking about them when they walked on the driveway.

Amber's work shows slivers of tiny mirror shards glued together. They dangle, waiting for a breeze to propel then like sails on a boat.

"Oh, definitely. I think the chimes is one of things that gave her the greatest joy."

"It looks a lot like what hung on the balcony at the restaurant in Chicago. Maybe she mixed the two up."

"I don't know. Mom didn't sound mixed up when she described them."

"And the brick. It looks so realistic."

"I don't know if that's the color that Mom saw in the house in Brampton. My prof showed me how to dab paint-paste to give the bricks that rough look. He gave me a small pad; you know the library stamp pads that says *paid*. Anyway, it gives the bricks a uniform size."

FACING REALITY

FOR JILL, JANUARY CRAWLS. Her time with Bill is reduced to Sunday suppers because Bill devotes his time to Mark. Jill continues the Friday suppers with the Croschuks but misses the Saturday-afternoon fireside talks with Bill. Mark joins Bill for the Sunday suppers, but the nature of their conversation is different. At the end of January, Jill joins Bill at the airport to say goodbye to Mark as he flies back to Saudi Arabia.

During the early part of January, Jill's hope of spending Saturdays with Julie wash out. Scott is home. Having completed his six-week stint up north, he has a three-week January break. While Scott is home, Julie quits her workouts. When Julie does call Jill, it is to ask if she would babysit. Scott has romantic dinner plans. The burning impression Jill wrestles with is she has nobody. Bill has Mark. Julie has Scott. Rebecca has Thomas. On Saturdays, Sarah works, and Matthew is involved in some church activity with his friends.

During the week, instead of an evening tea with Julie, Jill visits Gloria Brewster and a few of the other ladies from the Sunday school program. When they discuss plans for the Sunday school children, Jill hesitates to offer suggestions. She fears her input could lead to a substantial involvement. Such a commitment could interfere with the time she spends with Bill.

In February, Saturday fireside chats with Bill return. He seeks her thoughts about the clients at the Wellness Center. When she was in the hospital, she enjoyed those discussions. Frequently, Bill invites Jill to talk about her grandmother, a topic Jill loves. Over the course of the next two months, Jill tells Bill about Josey's house and the gardens. Later Jill's stories involve her past work with the Creative Arts Society of Brampton and her roommates, Linda Bryce and Karen Parkelle. Bill enjoys Jill's enthusiasm when she talks about her stage work. However, Jill doesn't tell Bill about her temporary lodging with Dave and Greg and with Mrs. Maxwell.

Through Bill's gentle probing, Jill reveals why she ran away from her grandmother. She lays the blame on a clever former boyfriend who was persistently hitting on her. Bill guesses Jill's relationship with Dave is not the cause for Jill's fear of returning to Oshawa. He explores another part of Jill's childhood by asking about the school drama projects. The moment he brings up Jill's home life, Jill conveniently changes the topic. When Bill asks about Jill's father, she abruptly tells him she doesn't want to talk about him. He drops his probing immediately, but he suspects he's found the reason why Jill is reluctant to visit her grandmother.

After Scott returns to the north, Julie joins Jill on evening workouts at the YWCA. Jill's efforts focus on cardio and muscle building. Their conversations center on their children. Then Julie shares Scott's intention to bring their family to see his parents early in July. She doesn't ask if Jill would join them on their trip to Ontario, but Jill's guilt rockets. She can't overcome a feeling that she would be running into trouble, more trouble than she could handle. The following week, Jill tells Julie that she won't be renewing her gym membership at the end of April. She explains that she no longer needs medication for her back and that working with Bill in his yard on Saturdays provides her with sufficient exercise.

For a break from turning over the soil and weeding some of the flower beds, Jill and Bill stroll around the yard, admiring the work they've done. Jill thinks about Josey and George working their yard in Brampton. *If only she could see me now*, wishes Jill. She imagines a nodding approval from her grandmother.

As they approach the patio, Bill's voice cuts in. "Something wrong?"

Jill looks up at Bill, trying to figure what gave rise to the question.

"For the last hour, you've been very quiet."

Jill doesn't know that three weeks ago, Julie met with Bill. Julie confessed she might have made an error by talking to Jill about returning to Ontario during their workouts. Julie admitted that she hoped her plans would spark a conversation about visiting Josey. Then Jill quit going to the YWCA. Since then, Julie initiates calls to Jill. It used to be Jill who always called her. Julie handed Bill a copy of an email she received from Kathy, Jill's sister.

The message described Kathy's perception of Josey as being very unhappy since Christmas. The staff at the senior facility made the same observation. Kathy's explanation was that Josey has nothing to look forward to. If Josey knew that Jill was coming to see her, Josey's whole outlook would change. Was there anything that Julie could do to get Jill to come down? She cautioned her request couldn't get back to Josey.

Answering Bill's question, Jill says, "I've been thinking about my grandmother."

"She must be quite a lady to hold your attention for so long."

"She is!"

"And you said she is ninety something?"

"Ninety-eight this year."

"Been around for some time. I expect she's very smart to have lasted so long."

"Yes."

"You figure she has many more years left?"

"I don't know."

"And yet you're willing to risk not going to see her while you can?"

Jill looks at Bill.

"You don't understand."

"Then help me understand."

Tears crawl out of Jill's eyes. She mumbles, "Hold me."

Bill steps closer and wraps his arms around Jill's limp frame. He stands, patiently holding her while she concentrates on the safety she finds in his firm grip. She rests in the warmth of his body.

Jill gathers strength to tell Bill about her reason for not returning to Ontario. Accepting his invitation to sit on one of the chairs on the patio, she wipes the pain away from her red eyes. A search of Bill's face shows no sign of rejection for her momentary weakness.

"When I lived at home, I often dreaded nights my father didn't come straight home from work. Those nights, Kathy and I would go to bed early."

"To sleep?"

"To hide."

"Usually it meant my father came home drunk. We hoped we didn't leave anything out to remind him of us. Sometimes we forgot something, a toy, a book, an article of clothing. If my mother didn't find it before he did, we'd hear him scream, 'Kathy!'

"He often blamed her for everything. It was like I didn't exist. Kathy would have to pick up whatever was left. Mom wasn't allowed to give it to her.

"She'd be lucky if he tried to kick her. He was so drunk he couldn't deliver any power, or he'd lose his balance. But, boy, if he got his hands on you. That would hurt. I know. When Kathy ran off, it was my name that he hollered. He'd pound you if you uttered a word.

"Once he was knocking Kathy around bad. I ran out of the bedroom and yelled at him. He glared at me and then charged like a bull. I think he tripped, but not before he rammed me into the wall. I fell to the floor dazed. I couldn't move. Mom screamed, claiming he killed me. That gave me an idea. I didn't move. I closed my eyes. Mom felt my pulse. 'She's alive. Call an ambulance.' Boy did that take the steam out of Father's rage." Jill chuckles.

"I waited for what I thought was five minutes. Then I groaned and opened my eyes. You'd think I would have thrown a scare into him so he wouldn't hit us again. Next time he came home, he hit Kathy. When he's drunk, he doesn't remember a thing."

Jill tells Bill the police were called several times, but it did no good. "Then he destroyed my drama project. I left. I said I would never return."

She looks at Bill, seeking his support. His silence leaves her to imagine that he is memorizing every detail of her story.

"Wow!" After a few moments, he says, "A very understandable reaction."

Jill nods, appreciating his response. The next moment, his brows wrinkle.

"And yet today, I would imagine your father must be somewhere in his midseventies, wouldn't you say?"

Jill guesses his implication. If her father is that old, how can he cause any harm? The absurdity of her position forces her to look down in shame. She searches for a more likely explanation for her fear. Not knowing what bothers her about her father overwhelms her. She feels stupid. The justification for not returning to Ontario gives way to a new disturbing revelation.

"His words," she mumbles.

Jill sees how her father's biting words—irresponsible, disobedient, willful, selfish, lazy, careless—burned her adolescent self-image. Rage boils within her. His accusing voice adds fuel to her fury. The red-faced image of her father appears and fades. An angry beast replaces it. Then she sees her face in the beast. The message shouts at Jill. Your reaction to his words will turn you into a monster like your father. The prospect burns like acid gnawing away her stomach.

Bill watches Jill digest the revelations his question initiates. He notes the narrowing of her red eyes, the tense cheek muscles, and her fingers curl, ready to scratch an opponent. Thinking about her reactions, he says, "Interesting."

Unaware of Bill's comment, a new disturbing revelation unsettles Jill. A way to avoid becoming an explosive person means preventing surprises, preventing shocks, controlling events. Thinking of her attempts to convince Daniel to have homeschooling, she wonders if he interpreted her efforts as controlling. *Could that be why Daniel thought I was selfish?* Jill's brows curl as she tries to better understand her son's behavior. *And Joseph? Could he have seen me as controlling?* The possibility that she is the cause for her marriage breakup causes her to shake her head. The possibility sticks in her memory like a sliver. Her eyes turn to Bill, searching for a hint that he too blames her. Instead, she sees him studying her, patiently waiting for something. *Did he ask me something?*

"I'm sorry. Where were we? I've forgotten what you were saying," she confesses.

"You were starting to say something about your father. Then you did a deep dive. Into your past, I imagine. I've been watching you try to work things out. Anything to share?"

Jill decides to keep them to herself. She guesses Bill may already know Daniel and Joseph's feelings, but she is not about to confirm them. That part of her history she intends to control. Trusting others can only compromise her strength. Bill's words "*trust me*" poke her like a finger of guilt.

Bill's chair scrapes the patio cement. Jill stands up. She watches him push her chair under the table too. Suspecting he has more to say, she prepares to challenge whatever he comes up with.

"The power of your father is greater than that of your grandmother," says Bill.

"You don't understand. I hate him. I don't ever want to see him again. I don't want to hear him attack me again." Jill feels her stomach muscles tighten. She adjusts her position, preparing to more forcefully defend herself.

Bill's relaxed posture doesn't change, forcing Jill to calm down. "Exactly. Your hatred for your father is more powerful than your love for your grandmother."

Jill's first impulse is to say, "What do you expect?" Her gut response upsets her. She pauses. *Oh no. I hate! Hate! That's like my father. Can't be. I left, so I wouldn't be like him.*

Rejecting her perceived insight, she searches for a more plausible reaction to her father. Bill's words "power of your father" nudge a disturbing conclusion.

I'm afraid of my father? How? Why?

No sooner do the questions surface than the answer dawns on her. The almost forgotten memories send a damp tremor through her. The words, "I'm afraid," spill out of her mouth.

"Afraid! Afraid of what?"

Jill is surprised to see Bill heard her. She thought she only mumbled. His attention on her is so focused that she knows she can't brush away her comment.

"Afraid of my father. Ever since I ran away from home, he's haunted me. I've had nightmares. I kept hearing him challenge what I've done, telling me that I will fail, laughing at me. It's like I can't get away from him."

The confession that tumbles from Jill's lips surprises her. She has never thought about the deep male voice in her dreams as her father speaking. Her words leave little doubt about their validity. Not wanting to go to Ontario now makes sense. She is afraid his malevolent spirit will find her again. The torturous attacks will begin again.

"If you ask me, those attacks, those accusations, it seems like the devil has been tormenting you," says Bill.

"That would be my father."

"You said *kept hearing.* That suggests a past. You aren't or haven't been hearing them lately."

Bill's revelation catches Jill by surprise. She thinks about it. She can't recall any nightmares after she gave up and took a bunch of pills. The male voice's prediction that her marriage will fail sends another shiver through Jill. *Is that the power I'm afraid of? His ability to make predictions, make predictions come true? Does he have that ability?* Jill sees her questions explaining another part of her fear of going to Ontario.

"Yes, I haven't had any recent nightmares."

"Why?"

"I feel more at peace."

"So what's changed?"

Jill thinks for some time. "My relationship with Daniel."

Bill nods.

"And you."

Bill smiles. "Earlier you said, '*I don't want to ever hear him attack me again.*'" Bill waits until he sees a questioning look on Jill's face. "I'd like to say that he can't say anything now that can hurt you?"

Jill shakes her head in disbelief.

"Is your self-image that fragile? Isn't what your grandmother thinks of you more important? What about your children? What about Julie's thoughts of you? What about *my* thoughts of you? Is your father's image more important than any of the people I mentioned or even all of them combined?"

"Bill, I'm afraid of what will happen when I see him. I don't want to take a chance that seeing him will bring on more nightmares. They're terrifying. You said pray about it. I did. Every night."

"And?"

"I've got no answer. I just have this vague impression that you should be with me, if I go to Ontario."

"And that's not enough?"

"I don't know. That's just the problem." Jill's voice shoots up an octave.

"Did I do a good job in helping you mend fences with Daniel?"

Jill nods.

"Then it's logical to conclude that I'll support you in every way if I come to Ontario with you?"

Jill nods again.

"Do you believe that God blessed you in how you dealt with Daniel?"

"I think so."

"Given that visiting your grandmother is an act of love, do you think it is likely that God will be with you in that effort?"

Jill nods.

"Good. Then all you have to do is pray that God will grant you the faith you need so you can undertake this mission with peace and confidence." He looks at Jill for some sign of objection. He sees none.

"And ask you to come with me?"

"That you can count on."

"You will come!"

"You bet. Who knows? We might even get to see Niagara Falls."

Jill smiles. "You don't mind if I make the arrangements, do you? I want to leave sometime early in August." Jill doesn't tell Bill that she wants to make sure they both have aisle seats. She remembers the issue they had on the Chicago flight. Also, they are to have separate hotel suites.

Bill agrees. "One more thing, if I may?"

"What?"

"I would suggest that you tell Julie your decision. I think she'd be very happy to hear it. I also expect that she'll let your grandmother know too. That'll probably make her day."

UNPREPARED

THE NEXT DAY AT church, Jill, bubbling with enthusiasm, tells Julie of her decision to visit her grandmother. Long-distance phone calls follow. On Monday, Jill books Bill and her flight to Toronto. Arrangements are made for a hotel and car rental. Jill's asks Bill if he is content with a midsize car. Bill knows from the tone of Jill's voice that sharing her excitement about the trip is the real reason for the call.

Her insurance settlement is signed. Because of her pain and suffering, she finds the payment very generous. The money covers more than the purchase of her car and her trip to Ontario.

As May nears its conclusion, the school's play becomes the main topic of conversation. Sarah drafts her all-too-willing mother into helping her memorize her lines. Amber cuts her holiday short to join the family for dress rehearsal. Bill promises to come. At Sarah's urging, Jill phones to invite Rebecca.

The call is difficult for Jill. Since Mark left for Saudi Arabia, she and Bill had slipped out of the habit of Friday-night suppers at the Croschuks. Rebecca is pleased to hear Jill's voice and to receive the invitation to the play. Her only request is that they come on Saturday instead of Friday night. Her explanation for Saturday saddens Jill. Thomas misses the times he spent at the farmer's market. He now looks for excuses to go to Camrose on Saturdays so he can visit vendors he knew for years. Jill has no trouble securing the change.

Amber's return home adds a new dimension to Jill's routine. Amber secures last year's construction job again and works long hours. With her sister home, Sarah's love for horseback riding returns. Every Sunday afternoon during the balance of the school year, they ride, and in the evening, they visit Daniel's family. Matthew, Jill, and Bill join the girls on their country trip. In July, while the girls make their weekly trips to the country, Bill, Jill, and sometimes Matthew spend every other Saturday at Bill's place.

Sarah's school play stirs old memories for Jill. The evening reminds Jill of when she attended drama classes in school. She dreamed someday of being a stage manager. Thinking of the August evenings she spent at the Brick Theater preparing for the play, *The Lion, the Witch, and the Wardrobe* spikes a hunger for rejoining the community drama club, but her job prevents her from attending their afternoon meetings.

On the second Sunday before their flight to Toronto, Jill is unusually quiet. Bill waits until Matthew has left to see his friends. Then he and Jill take their regular walk to the neighborhood park.

As they near the park, he asks, "Something wrong?"

"I'm worried."

"About going to see your family in Ontario?"

"Not the family." Jill explains she's had several phone calls with Kathy and Josey. She is looking forward to seeing them. "It's something about going back to Oshawa."

"Cold feet."

"Maybe. I can't figure out why. Going back feels like I'm going to be arrested, like there's a bench warrant out for me failing to go to court. I have to face the judge, but I don't know what I've done wrong."

Jill glances at Bill, searching for a hint of disapproval.

"Could it be guilt for running out on your grandmother?"

"No. It feels more serious than that. At the same time, I think I don't deserve to be hauled into court. Crazy! Isn't it?"

"Puzzling." He notes the tension in Jill's voice.

Jill stops walking and faces Bill. "Let me try and explain it this way. One spring afternoon, I was driving Joseph's truck to pick him up from the market. I stepped on the brakes and started sliding into the intersection. I decided I'd end up in the middle, so I drove right through. I didn't think anything of it until a ticket came in the mail. The picture showed me driving. Joseph said he'd pay the fine and be done with it. I objected. The roads were very slippery. I couldn't help it. I wasn't driving *without due care and caution*. Anyway, I went to court. Have you ever gone to court?" Jill looks again at Bill.

He shakes his head.

"It's scary. At least for me it is. I watched the judge lecture three accused people before me. Words like *road safety, watch out for others, you're not the only one on the road*, accused the people before me of being immature, irresponsible. The last guy, a young guy, was even told to *grow up*. The judge seemed to be on a mission, crucify poor drivers."

She doesn't tell Bill that the judge's attacks reminded her of her father.

"Then it was my turn. I'm sure he saw me shaking like a leaf in the wind. He smiled and helped me explain why I came to court. My only defense was to describe the nature of the roads. I presented a copy of a newspaper article describing the roads and weather at the time. I had no other evidence. I knew it was wrong to drive through the intersection on a red light. I deserved to be punished. In the end, he reduced the charge and the fine. The point I'm trying to make is that when I was looking up at him, I felt like a little mouse trapped. The cat was a foot away. Anyway, that's the feeling I have about going back to Ontario. I've tried to figure out what I've done wrong. The only thing I can come up with is running away from home."

"If that's all it is, then I don't think you have anything to worry about. I doubt you'll be charged or fined." Bill smiles, a smile that reminds Jill of the judge's sympathetic smile.

"I hope you're right."

JOSEY'S REVELATION

NERVOUSLY, JILL DRIVES THE rental car up to the iron bar gates of McKenzie Manor. She adjusts the rearview mirror to check her hair. It's perfect, styled as her mother had done. Jill hopes to impress Josey. Leaning out of her window, she presses the speaker button.

"Please state your name and purpose for entry."

"Jill Kreshky to see Josey Sommerfeld."

"You're expected. Welcome to our facility."

While Jill waits for the gates to open, she gazes around at the huge brick complex. At the far end of the parking lot is a six-floor structure with a wide canopy to greet guests. On both sides of the entrance, three-story wings extend like welcoming arms. The left wing is more than twice as long as the right, but the right wing's brick is a lighter tint than the rest of the building. *Recent construction.*

As Jill rolls down the driveway, three narrow lanes open up along the right side of the parking lot. Single-floor and one- and two-bedroom cottages line one side of the lane. Lanterns on the other side stand ready to light up a cement walkway. Jill crawls along the driveway to a parking space at the far end of the parking lot. She reads the names over the entrances to each wing: Masters Manor, Maidens Manor, and Main Manor. Josey is in Main Manor.

Wide glass doors await Jill's arrival. A motion detector signals first the exterior and then the interior glass doors to part. As she slowly passes through, a large open space welcomes her. To her right is an area with end tables and several couches and armchairs. Jill estimates it could accommodate two dozen people. To her left is a counter behind which are two middle-aged women. One woman is working at a computer and is almost hidden. The second woman, with short red hair and silver glasses, is standing and looking at Jill.

"First time here?" she says with a smile.

Jill nods. She realizes she is standing like a misplaced piece of furniture. Jill's first impression is she is in the wrong building. The entrance suggests a luxury hotel. A light-yellow maple second-floor railing circles the huge foyer. Set well back from the railing are doors, entrances to people's suites. This place in no way resembles the seniors facility in which Mary and Ed live. It is more like the registration center at the Chicago conference center.

"How may I help you?" The woman's welcoming smile draws Jill to the counter.

Not wanting to broadcast that she has walked into the wrong place, Jill says in a low voice, "I'm here to see Mrs. Sommerfeld."

"Josey. Yes. Would you be Jill Kreshky?"

"I am." Jill wonders if she needs to present identification. She begins to open her purse.

"Wonderful. Welcome to McKenzie Manor. Josey is expecting you." She glances down as she jots the room number on a Main Manor slip of paper. When she looks up again, she says, "Josey is in suite 604. Turn right after you leave the elevator. Your grandmother's door is the second one on your left." She hands Jill the paper. Seeing Jill appear lost, she adds, "The elevators are behind this welcome center."

"Thank you."

"I hope you don't mind. I'd like to call Josey and let her know you are on the way up," says the red-haired woman.

"No problem." Still feeling out of place, Jill slowly walks away from the counter. After rounding the corner, she finds the elevators.

Jill knocks twice on the door at 604 before it opens. It swings in faster than she expects. The lady inside is shorter than Jill remembers. Wrinkles line her face, but Jill recognizes Josey's joyful smile. Seeing thin, shaking hands, Jill expects weak, slow movement, but an ascending, advancing cathead cane in one hand dispels that notion. In seconds, Josey's strong arms wrap around her. Jill responds, putting her right arm around Josey and extending the left arm to stop the door from hitting her grandmother in the back.

"Jill, I'm so glad you came. It's an answer to my prayer. Come in, dear.

Come in." Josey steps back, and with the help of her cane she leads Jill to the kitchen table. "Tea?"

The sound of Josey's voice is exactly as Jill remembers it, strong, confident, and directing. Jill follows her slow-moving grandmother, and she scans the unit—a large open kitchen–living room; to the right by the entrance is the washroom. A second door Jill guesses is to Josey's bedroom. A thirty-six-inch LED television screen hangs on the wall opposite a love seat. A chair on casters is pulled away from a desk holding a seventeen-inch Macintosh computer screen.

Josey takes some cups and a plate of brownies from the cupboard and sets them on the table. She notes Jill's face light up. "Yes, the brownies have walnuts."

"You remembered!" Jill beams as she selects one of the largest squares. Walnuts in her brownies, Jill's favorite, something her sister objected to.

"Some things never change," says Josey. "You're punctual, like you always were. I like your hair. It's like your mother styled it. Only then, your hair used to hide your face." She chuckles, pleased her memories return so easily.

Josey sets a pot of tea on the table and sits down. She notes how carefully Jill nibbles on her favorite treat and guesses Jill is a little uncomfortable. After pouring the tea, Josey begins by sharing highlights from her life. She avoids any topics she suspects are sensitive, like how and when she found Jill's sister or anything about her mother's illness. Josey avoids telling Jill about her heart event five years ago. Even Julie doesn't know that Josey needed two stents. When she feels Jill is relaxed enough, she asks about Jill's children.

Jill dives into Amber's painting successes. She proudly announces that Amber is in a fine arts program at the University of Alberta and predicts someday Amber will be famous. When she talks about Sarah and her interest in drama, she notes it isn't a passion like Amber's art fascination. Neither is Sarah's two career interests—dietician or pharmacist. Matthew, she describes as loving team sports. He is an honor student like Daniel. When she talks about her oldest son, Jill's attention focuses on his present family—Eve, Sharon, Shelly, Shannon, and Shawn.

"I'm a great-grandmother!" rejoices Josey. "Oh, how I wish they could have come too." For Josey, her exclamation is one of pride not surprise. She had already learned of the grandchildren from Julie. Josey also notices that Jill skips saying anything about Joseph, their divorce, or the tension that existed between her and Daniel.

"Oh, Eve gave me one of her photo albums to show you," says Jill. "It's at the hotel. I'll bring it next time."

"Wonderful. I'd love to see it."

"I also brought two albums of my children growing up and your album that you sent down with Julie."

"Tell me about my great-grandchildren."

Jill draws on the times Daniel and his family came over to her place and when she visited them. As the stories tumble out, Josey determines that she hasn't ever seen Jill so happy.

"Julie told me something about you being in a car accident and being in the hospital for some time." Josey studies Jill to detect any change in demeanor. None appears.

Jill immediately launches into her time at the hospital, telling about situations with which Josey can relate. Josey's heart attack continues to remain a secret. She smiles when Jill includes Bill's hospital visits. Without any additional prompting, Jill describes several times that she and Bill did things together, like finding her new car. Josey is impressed with the enthusiasm that marks Jill's account. She judges her passion for Bill is about the same as her feelings for Amber.

"And where is this mystery man?"

"At the hotel, suntanning near the pool."

"You left him there by himself! You should have brought him."

"It was his idea," objects Jill, concerned she may look inconsiderate. "He thought we might want some time alone."

Josey glances at her watch. "It's almost lunchtime. Why don't you call him? See if he would like two lovely ladies to join him. I want to meet him. We can eat there. That'll give me a chance to get out of this place. You know I hardly go out." She almost said, "Since I lost my driver's license." The doctor said it was unlikely that she would pass out anymore. Josey accepted his declaration that her license should be canceled. She was afraid to get behind the wheel. Her three-year-old Cadillac sold without any trouble. She now relies on Kathy or a taxi.

In three-quarters of an hour, all three gather around a table and order lunch. Josey's questions dig into Bill's past. When she asks about his future, she finds him vague. In observing the actions between Jill and Bill, she notes little intimacy in their words or actions. This puzzles her. From Jill's earlier conversation, she expects more signs of familiarity.

Not wanting to give away her curiosity, she switches topics. "Jill, have you given any thought to seeing the house you spent one summer at? You know, the one in Brampton."

"Yes. I was hoping to go and see it. I haven't said anything to Bill." She looks at Bill for his reaction. Seeing him look interested, she continues, "I didn't know if you still owned it and if you did, how you would feel about me taking a look at it."

"Wonderful!" Josey leans forward in anticipation. "Maybe you could do me a favor."

"What?"

"When you go, I would like you to pretend you are interested in purchasing the property. I'll put you in touch with my property manager. He'll show you the place. The tenants who are there, and they have been there for six years, have been requesting several improvements in the house. Some reasonable, but other upgrades are a bit much. At least that's what Marvin says. Marvin's my manager. He has the list of their requests. Tell me which you think should be done. You know, if you owned the property, what would you do?"

"Wouldn't posing as prospect buyers make the tenants nervous?" asks Bill.

Josey beams and chuckles. "Precisely. It might also lower their expectations."

"That's great!" Jill sees this as an opportunity to go through the whole house. Her earlier hopes were to drive by the place. Maybe talk to the people living there and see a bit of the house.

"So when do you see yourselves going? I should give the tenants some notice."

Bill looks at Jill and says, "You're meeting with your sister tomorrow, so why don't we drive to Brampton the day after tomorrow?"

Jill agrees.

Bill turns to Josey. "Want to come?"

"Oh no. I don't care to sit in a car for that long anymore. You two go and report to me later. I'd like to hear from both of you too."

After they finish their dessert, Bill asks to use the car for the afternoon. He wants to explore Oshawa for two or three hours. Looking at Josey, Jill suggests they enjoy the albums she brought. Josey takes a sip of water as she swallows her pain pills and considers her response. Reluctantly, she agrees to Jill's proposal.

As Bill stands to leave, Josey feels her hopes of talking to Bill privately are slipping away. She wants to know Bill more as a person, to know his feelings toward her granddaughter too. Even more, she wants Bill's thoughts on how he sees Jill's doing. She suspects Julie may not have told her everything about Jill. She also wants to compare the information she has received from Jill's pastor. Before Bill walks too far away, Josey calls him back.

"Bill, if you aren't doing anything tomorrow morning, when Jill is with Kathy, why don't you come and visit me for a while? I can show you the place I live at. That's if you're not doing anything?"

Bill agrees.

Josey and Jill leave the restaurant and head for the pool. Josey points her cane to a table far away from other hotel guests. She sets a pace considerably slower than this morning's, leading Jill to believe Josey is in pain. Not wanting to highlight her grandmother's discomfort, Jill accepts the crawl pace. It reminds her of when she first started walking in the hospital. When they reach the table, Jill considers rushing to her room for the albums, but Josey points to the chair next to her. Jill finds her action strange. In Josey's suite and in the restaurant, Josey sat in the chair across the table from Jill. Now she directs Jill to sit next to her.

As Jill follows her grandmother's request, she says, "I'm so glad you asked us to see your place in Brampton. You know I've never forgotten it. I loved it. You have always been so good to me. You're the absolute best." Jill holds her grandmother's hand.

"I love you too, dear," begins Josey, "but I'm afraid I'm not as good as you think. In fact, I've done some things in the past that I really regret, some things that I think are responsible for some of the troubles that you have experienced. I hope you will be able to forgive me."

Jill's hand slips back. "No, Josey. You have always been more than kind to me."

"You need to hear me out, dear. Hear my whole story. It's a story that I didn't appreciate until I visited your mom in the hospital." She pauses and looks at Jill's face before spilling out the rest of her information. "I wasn't very fair to your father."

Jill takes a breath to object, but says nothing when she sees her grandmother shake her head.

"When your mom started going out with Frank, I didn't approve. He drank. He came home late from parties. I mean, when he can't get up for an eleven o'clock church service, you know he was out too late."

Jill nods.

"Then your mother started falling into his patterns of missing church. I put my foot down. It didn't help. She married him. For a while, I thought Frank might change. At first, Janet had him coming to church regularly. I think I spoiled that. When the minister preached about self-control or the dangers of drinking, I made a point of drawing it to Frank's attention."

"Janet?" asks Jill, her brow wrinkled.

"I'm sorry. I should have said Alice." Josey shakes her head. "Your mother's full name is Janet Alice Rezley. Calling your mother Alice was one of the ways Frank told me that Alice was part of his family and not mine."

Jill nods as she recalls Julie telling her about that when she and Julie first met.

"Let me get back to my story. It will all make sense when I finish."

With Jill's nod, she continues.

"Now, let see. Where was I? Oh yes. Frank quit going to church. Next thing I hear, he quit his job as a mechanic. He worked at some corner service station in Brampton. They moved to Oshawa, where he got a job in the General Motors plant. For a while, I had no idea where they went until Janet—I mean Alice—phoned me. Frank's excuse to Alice was the new job paid better. I think he wanted to avoid running into me or at least me knowing what he was up to."

Josey's quivering voice and shaking hands prompt Jill to suggest that Josey stop for a rest.

"It was a very stressful time for me," Josey admits. The idea that Frank successfully escaped her critical eye forced Josey to admit that he would never change. She thought that Frank had every intention of wasting his money on parties and drinking.

Josey takes a deep breath and grips her hands firmly. "Let me continue, please," she says when her hands quit shaking. "I really need you to hear the rest of the story."

Jill notes the change in tone of her grandmother's voice. She isn't telling Jill. She's asking, almost begging.

"If you're sure."

"For three years, I had to settle for long-distance calls to my daughter. Then George, Joey's husband, had an opportunity to move to Oshawa too. His company was opening up a new office there. I convinced George to accept. Before long, Alice and I began seeing each other. After a while, Frank would come with Alice to our house for dinner. Not often, mind you, but he would show up, for special occasions."

Jill nods. Her thoughts turn to the stressful times she endured when Daniel married and moved out to the country. On special occasions, he'd come to her house too. The fact that Josey experienced a similar situation comforts Jill. She suspects Josey would understand the tension between her and Daniel.

"About two years later, Alice became pregnant. Before I knew it, Joyce Kathy was born. I was a grandmother. I was so happy."

"I thought my sister's name was Kathy Joyce?"

"No. When she was baptized, it was Joyce Kathy," corrects Josey confidently. "Hang on. I'll explain. After the baptism, Frank came to church with Alice. I began to think that being a father was changing him. Later, I learned that he was drinking less and coming home earlier. I didn't needle him about his drinking. I learned my lesson."

"Wait a minute. Did Mom tell you that my father was drinking less?"

"Oh no. That was a touchy subject. Alice and I didn't discuss that. I knew a number of women whose husbands worked at the GM plant and had the same shift as Frank. They were my grapevine. They kept me well informed. For instance, I knew that Frank was being considered for a promotion. One of the supervisors fell seriously ill, and Frank's name came up as a replacement. Frank was known for quality work. He also had a talent for teaching new procedures to men and encouraging them to accept changes."

"You knowing that shouldn't have been a problem," says Jill.

"It wasn't, but I also found out when Frank drank heavily. One night, when he left the bar, he backed into a metal railing, damaging the passenger's side of his car. I waited until his day off to visit Alice. It was only three days later. Frank hadn't booked the vehicle with a body shop yet. Of course, I drew his attention to the damage. He tried to brush it off by saying it was just a little accident. I said, '*An accident fueled by alcohol.*' That was my mistake."

"What do you mean?"

"I let it slip that I had heard all about the accident. I exposed my grapevine. He was furious. Said I was spying on him. I had no right. I challenged him. We argued. We got into a shouting match. I said things I shouldn't have."

"Like?" Jill leaned forward, hungry for dirt on her father.

"Like if word got out about his drinking, he might not get the promotion. He took that as a threat. Boy, did he explode! Told me to quit interfering in his life."

Memories of her father's temper, his yelling at Jill's mother, surface. Instinctively, Jill tenses. She expects to hear that Frank turned violent. Jill looks carefully at her grandmother. Josey is now in full control of her hands. There's no shaking. Her fighting spirit makes her twenty years younger.

"I think what did it was me telling him that I didn't think he was fit to be a good husband. My predicting he would turn out to be a poor father shocked him. At first, he tried to defend himself. Said he would always provide for his family. Then he gave up on that. Instead, he told me to—and I quote—'*Get the hell out and never come back. And don't ever try to talk or in any other way communicate with anyone in this family.*'"

"Seriously?"

"Oh yes. He was very serious. I couldn't phone your mother, send her birthday or Christmas cards, nothing."

"How would he know if you phoned?"

"That's what we thought. For half a year after that, I phoned Alice when Frank was at work. Then one day, your mother said something that clued him in. Was he angry! That's when he made it clear that your mother was supposed to completely forget about me, that I was not part of the family. To remind her, he began calling her Alice, instead of Janet, and your sister Kathy. He knew about our tradition of having family names starting with J. I guess he thought by dropping that tradition, your mother would know he was serious."

"And what if Mom wouldn't have gone along with it?"

"Your mother said he threatened to quit his job and move somewhere else. Maybe it was an idle threat, but Alice didn't want to take a chance. Her financial situation was so much better than when Frank worked at the service station."

"But my name starts with a J."

"Remember, you were born five years after Kathy. Maybe Frank cooled down. Maybe your mother developed more of a backbone. I don't really know. My information came filtered through my grapevine. I do know that your mother insisted on going to church. She had to go to a church farther away, but she did take you girls with her."

"At the beginning, you said you wanted me to forgive you. What for? My father's drinking was a choice he made. You couldn't do anything about it? You even tried."

Jill rubs the back of her head and neck. The tension and the subsequent headache that she used to experience while living at home begins to grip her. She recalls the hopelessness of trying to reason with her father. It's part of the reason why she ran away.

"I was wrong. I overplayed my hand," says Josey. "By pushing too hard, I lost touch with you and Kathy and your mother. You couldn't get to know me. It was my fault. I considered trying to see you and Kathy, maybe at school or something, but I knew if Frank ever found out, he might carry out his threat. At least, as things stood, I worked my grapevine. And as far as I could tell, Frank kept his word. He did provide for all of you."

Jill slides her chair closer to Josey and wraps her arm around her grandmother. "There's nothing to forgive. You meant well. It isn't your fault that you tried too hard to protect us. Really, your heart was in the right place."

Josey pats Jill's hand. "It's so kind of you to say that. Julie has told me how highly you think of me. I was afraid if I died without you knowing the truth, you would see me as a fraud."

"Josey, you were there for me when I really needed you, even though I hardly knew you. I couldn't even call you Gramma. You rescued me by saying I should call you Josey. That was such a special time. I could never think of you as anything but the best."

"There is another thing," says Josey.

Jill sits back, wondering what more Josey could confess.

"I told you how my blindness about your father's drinking caused me to adopt a poor strategy of dealing with him. Well, his drinking blinded me to seeing that outside of his drinking, he was a good man."

Jill's mouth drops.

"No. Hear me out," says Josey as she shakes her head to stop Jill's objection. "Like you, I wouldn't have thought so. Especially two months after you left Brampton and Alice phoned and told me she was leaving Frank. I set her up in an apartment near me so we could spend time together. I covered whatever she couldn't pay so she wouldn't turn to Frank. I made her promise she would never tell Frank where she lived. And bless her, she didn't. What I didn't know is that she still kept in touch with him. If I had known at the time that she was phoning him, I would have said she was crazy. She saw something good in him that I couldn't or didn't want to. I can't even say I know what it was.

"Then Alice became ill. There were tests and tests and tests. Eventually, we learned she had lung cancer. When she was hospitalized, Frank spent every minute that he wasn't at work with her. Near the end, he took a long-term leave and stayed with Alice day and night. What surprised me is he quit drinking. Quit smoking too. Completely. No stepping out for a drag and then returning. One of the times that I convinced Frank to go downstairs and get something to eat, Alice explained his changed behavior. She said Frank was praying for her recovery. He promised God that if she recovered, he would never touch another cigarette or drink again."

Guessing what Jill was about to say, Josey says, "Yes, yes, I know. That wouldn't turn things around. Alice said she thought it was his way of saying that he would do anything to help her. '*He really does love me*,' your mom said. I let my bias about his drinking blind me to the possibility that he was capable of any love. I didn't think he had it in him."

He loved her! Mom loved him. Impossible, thinks Jill.

"When I first saw him adopt his abstinence role, I thought he was trying to punish himself."

"Punish himself! For what?" Jill leans forward, eager for an explanation.

"His smoking. I thought he blamed himself for Alice getting lung cancer because he smoked. Maybe that's the case. I don't know, but I suspected that was his motivation."

"But you don't think so any longer?"

"The time I saw him at the hospital, he seemed to be a completely changed man. He was considerate, caring. No hint of anger. It's almost like he reverted to the time when he was courting her. Maybe he realized he was about to lose the most important thing in his life. I honestly think if he could have traded places with her, he would have."

In response to Jill's look of surprise, Josey says, "Yes. Me too. I found it hard to believe. I guess you had to be there to see it."

Jill shakes her head in disbelief. *This is not the man I knew. Maybe Josey was not in a clear emotional frame of mind to assess Father accurately.*

"I don't blame you for not believing me," says Josey. "Maybe you'll believe Kathy. Her opinion of him changed too."

"Kathy was there?"

"Yes. When I knew how serious Alice's situation was, I hired detectives to search for you and Kathy. Detective Davidson couldn't find you. He suspected you lived somewhere in Camrose, but he couldn't get any clearer information. Detective Coatels found Kathy. She was working in Toronto at the time. Kathy came at once. She spent more time in the hospital than I did. That's how she got to know your father better."

"Do you know what happened to him?"

"All I know is he stayed around for the funeral. Then I lost track of him. I heard rumors, but I didn't care to check them out. I know he kept in touch with Kathy. If you ask her, I'm sure she'll give you a clearer picture of what happened to him."

"I'm really looking forward to seeing my sister. I haven't seen her in so long."

Josey welcomes Jill's happy demeanor. "I know she's looking forward to seeing you tomorrow too. Speaking of looking forward, I want to see those pictures of my great-grandchildren. Didn't you say you have an album to show me?"

Josey declines Jill's invitation to come up. She's tired. "If we sit here, it will be easier for Bill to spot us." Bill promised to drive her to her apartment when he returned. Jill goes to her suite and gets the album.

Together, they spend the afternoon viewing Eve's album. Josey enjoys Jill's stories about the children as much as she does the photos. At one point, Jill catches tears running down Josey's face.

"I missed all that with you and Kathy," says Josey. "Don't ever allow that connection to break between you and your grandchildren. I learned my lesson too late."

Jill is thankful that she apologized to Daniel before she came to see her grandmother. She plans to thank Bill again for his help. *I hate to think what Josey would have thought of me if I hadn't patched things up with Daniel.*

When Bill returns, Josey quickly accepts his offer to drive her home. Jill goes to her suite for a rest and to change for supper. During their meal, Jill is quiet. While she drinks a glass of wine by the pool, Bill encourages Jill to share what's troubling her. She changes the subject. When Jill finishes her glass of wine, she excuses herself and goes to her suite.

The possibility that Jill's father is not the kind of man that Jill remembers bothers her. Was her assessment of him incorrect? Did he change? Reviewing her memories of him, she confirms he was mean, even dangerous. Jill dares to wonder if she was the cause of her father's irritation. She remembers her nightmares, the deep, growling male voice. She suspects her father's spirit came to torture her. *He hates me.*

Her thoughts shift to her sister. Once again, Jill feels abandoned by her sister. *How can Kathy think my father wasn't mean? She ran away from him too. How could she keep in touch with him after Mom died?*

Jill goes to bed early. To distract herself, she turns the radio on, hoping the music will divert her thoughts. Maybe the announcer's news, his jokes, would bring her into the present. It doesn't, but sleep rescues Jill.

In the morning, Jill relaxes, thankful she experienced no nightmare. She tries to recall the last time a nightmare plagued her. After a while, she thinks the last time she heard the victorious male laughter was when Joseph left her. The prediction that her marriage to Joseph wouldn't last still sends a chill through Jill. Her willpower didn't save the marriage. Admitting she failed leads Jill to think that she doesn't have the power to assure herself of her own commitments. Feeling vulnerable sends a cold chill through her. *I need to be more vigilant, be ready to escape instantly.* She goes to the restaurant for breakfast without stopping to ask if Bill will join her. Doubts about her future haunt her until she hears Bill's cheerful voice.

"Hey! There you are. Did you forget about me?" He quickly walks up to her table but pauses momentarily.

"No. I just needed some time for myself." Seeing Bill's hesitation, she indicates he should join her.

"Something wrong?" He sits down.

Hiding behind the excuse that she hasn't seen her sister in a long time, Jill asks, "Do you think Kathy will be angry with me for not trying to get in touch?"

"Absolutely not. She'll be thrilled to see you." The confident tone of his voice dismisses Jill's fears. "From what I understand, you had no idea about where she lived."

Jill pushes her empty fruit bowl away and starts on her cereal. The waitress takes Bill's order of French toast, three strips of crisp bacon, and a side order of ham. He also orders a cup of tea, something he has started drinking for breakfast since he met Jill. While he waits for his order, he prods Jill for more information about Josey.

Josey's pride on being well informed leads him to suspect that when he goes to visit her later in the morning, he'll be under her microscope. By questioning Jill about Josey's relationship with Kathy, he hopes to garner an idea of what Josey expects from him.

Before Bill flew to Oshawa, he'd done an internet search on the Sommerfeld background. He'd learned that Josey's husband, George, originally was connected with the railroad. Later, dabbling in commercial real estate investment, he amassed a huge fortune. For the last couple of decades, Josey's heavy involvement in philanthropic ventures earned her respect from many people and organizations.

Yesterday, he visited a few of the charities with which Josey was associated. Admiration for Josey's financial, promotional, and organizational talents echoed over and over. She did everything from financing and directing to hands-on work. The people Bill talked to all believed Josey's energy suggested she was at least ten years younger than her actual age.

Bill suspects Josey will have high expectations of anyone who wishes to be involved with her granddaughter. Impressing Josey could be a major bonus. If she lets Jill know she approves of Bill, then there would be a greater chance that Jill would accept his marriage proposal. He knows his hinting about Niagara Falls as being a honeymoon capital has fallen short. Jill hasn't even considered the possibility that they might spend the rest of their days together.

The possibility of Jill agreeing to marriage also depends upon her dealing with the ghosts in her past, ghosts that Bill suspects reside in Ontario. Jill, asking him to come with her, leads Bill to believe that she expects a strong challenge. She may even turn to him for help. When Jill faces that skeleton, he believes she'll be open to completely trusting him. Being available, patient, and supportive are the keys he's counting on to open her heart.

During his morning visit, he hopes to learn about Jill's past. Any information could be helpful in supporting Jill. But winning Josey's trust means he must earn her respect. He counts on his dedication to Jill as his trump card.

After breakfast, Jill returns to her room to change. Bill waits for her in the hotel foyer.

"Well, what do you think?" Jill's spirited greeting catches him by surprise. His hand indicates she should turn around again.

Her white-cuffed capris, which she purchased before their trip, catch his eye first. The low-cut light-blue top flashes by as she turns. Her ponytail, poking out from the back of her white cap, sails out as if it seeks to be free. A light-blue sweater with a white swirl sweeping down drapes her shoulder. Bill's eye drops to the sandals. Toenails are painted, a first.

Seeing Bill frown when his eye sees the sandals, Jill explains, "Trying to look my best."

Bill gives Jill two thumbs up. "Accompanying you makes me feel ten years younger." He doesn't tell her that her most outstanding feature is her energetic, optimistic nature.

KATHY'S REVELATIONS

When they arrive at McKenzie Manor and walk through the interior glass doors, Laura, the woman with short red hair and silver glasses, waves Jill on to the elevators. She also calls up to Josey's suite to let her know her other granddaughter has arrived. Jill and Bill ride up to the sixth floor in silence, each anticipating what is to come.

The elevator door opens, and a lady about Jill's age stands with arms outstretched. As if someone at a race said *go*, they both rush to each other, saying their sister's name. Arms wrap around each other. In unison, they each say, "It's been too long." Drawing away for a moment, they laugh at their responses. Tears flow from their eyes. Then they hug again.

Bill prevents the elevator door from closing until the buzzer sounds. Together, they move into the hall. Jill initiates introductions.

Josey cuts in by recommending the girls be off. "You two have a lot of catching up to do." She directs Jill to press the button for the elevator. "And Bill is going to treat me to a tea and a bran muffin in the cafeteria downstairs, aren't you?" She looks at Bill, expecting his approval.

As they get off on the main floor, Jill overhears Josey saying with a gentle laugh, "So, Bill, you have to tell me how it is that you get away with masquerading as a psychologist at the Wellness Center in Camrose."

"You've been talking to someone at the Wellness Center?"

"Your Reverend Williams. He tells me you're not half bad either." With her right hand on her cane, she tucks her left hand in the crook of Bill's extended arm. The next moment, her cane points him in the direction of the cafeteria.

Jill struggles to hear Bill's response, but the sound of the opening of the interior glass doors of Main Manor drowns him out. Kathy directs her sister to a two-door sky-blue 2010 Cougar. With a toss of her purse, she climbs in. Jill follows her lead. In response to Jill's question of where they are going, she tells Jill she knows just the mall for shopping.

The morning's window-shopping is the setting Kathy uses to hit on the highlights of her last thirty plus years. She describes meeting Larry, her husband, and his involvement with the children. She describes the holidays and dinner theaters they attended before moving to Markham from Toronto. The achievements of Joyce, her twenty-one-year-old daughter, and Jack, who is nineteen years old, betray an unrestrained pride in her children. Both have won scholarships and are attending universities in the States.

At lunch, Kathy digs into Jill's family history. Jill begins by describing Amber's interest in painting, Sarah's involvement in the theater and dreams to be a dietician or pharmacist, and Matthew's honors standing and interest in sports. She praises Daniel in selecting Eve, a loving wife and mother. She promises to show Kathy the scrapbook of her grandchildren. When Kathy asks about Joseph, Jill dismisses it as a time she wants to forget.

Wishing to change the subject, Kathy comments on how Daniel is following the family custom in naming the children. "He is using the *sh* instead of the *j* sound. How is it that you dropped our tradition?"

Jill's response was fast. "I guess I didn't feel any real attachment to my family then." Her thoughts flash to the night her father broke her drama assignment. Her mother's words, "*She has a mind of her own. Yes, there's no controlling her.*" The words still bite. Noticing that her remark darkens Kathy's face, Jill senses criticism coming. She points out that Kathy had an equal dislike for their parents. "We were both of the same mind. Why did you change?"

"Perhaps what you'll see next will help you understand." Having finished lunch, Kathy asks for the bill.

"Where we going?"

Kathy walks to the till. "A place not too far away." Kathy's paying for the lunch interrupts Jill's questioning. When they walk outside, Kathy talks about the time she spent in the hospital with her mother. Much of what Kathy relates, Jill has already heard from Josey. Jill listens patiently, searching for some hint as to why Kathy altered her thoughts about her parents.

"Now I realize that Josey may have told you some of what I've said …" She glances at Jill as she turns into a cemetery.

Jill nods in response.

"I wanted you to be on the same page as I am, so you will better understand what Mom asked me to do."

After winding down some narrow paths, Kathy pulls over and quietly walks among the headstones until she stands before a pair of headstones, cement structures that, seen together, appear like the outline of a house. Kathy stands back as Jill steps closer and reads the inscription.

JANET ALICE REZLEY
rests in peace
1935–1981

Love
is patient … is kind …
keeps no record of wrongs …
always protects,
always trusts,
always hopes,
always perseveres
1 Cor. 13:4–7

Beneath Janet's name is a sketched partially opened rosebud. Jill's eye follows the stem angling more horizontally than down. A second stem rises up from the Bible passage, mirroring the top stem. The passage appears on an open right side page in the Bible.

Tears flow. Jill realizes her love of roses grows out of something her mother shared. After drying her eyes, Jill steps back and looks at her sister. Kathy points to the stone next to Janet's. Jill turns and looks where Kathy points. Her hand sweeps to her mouth. There's a mirror image headstone, complete with the same inscription and rose sketches. A vase between the two headstones holds a large bouquet of artificial flowers.

FRANK REZLEY
rests in peace
1930–2009

Love
is patient … is kind …
keeps no record of wrongs …
always protects,
always trusts,
always hopes,
always perseveres
1 Cor. 13:4–7

Jill stands frozen, staring at her father's grave. She can't believe the source of her fear is no longer alive. She feels a weight removed from her back. Still, she remains tense. The idea that he could die seems impossible, but the evidence persists. A gentle hand rests on her right shoulder. Kathy's whisper in her left ear draws Jill out of a trance.

"Let's sit down." Kathy points to a bench several feet away. With her arm around Jill, she herds her sister. Once they are both firmly seated, Kathy begins.

"Mom loved Father. She said a year after he graduated, he was recognized as a talented mechanic. He had a passion for his work. His energy and fun-loving spirit soared. Before that, in high school, he was an ordinary guy. He caught no one's eye except Mom's."

"But he drank so much." Jill suspects an exaggeration, if not an ignoring of facts.

"Mom said he knew his limits and kept to them too, at least until after I was born." Kathy's silence causes Jill to look up from the grass. She studies her sister's serious face.

"Jill, what I'm going to tell you next you can't tell another living soul."

Jill's puzzled look nudges Kathy's explanation.

"I promised Mom I would tell no one else but you. Mom insisted if I told you, you would first have to promise to tell no one else. She doesn't want this to get back to Josey."

Jill quickly agrees and adjusts her body to face her sister.

"Mom told me that at heart Father had an inferiority complex. It mostly disappeared when he became known as a wizard with engines. That changed a few years after I was born. He doubted he was a good father …"

Frank began comparing himself with other fathers at work. The ones who caught his ear were men who had sons, sons who were older and could horse around with their father in various sports activities. In his mind, taking his daughter to church, out for ice cream, or to the show were nonevents. Frank had nothing to share with his fellow workers. Kathy didn't play piano, dance, or sing. He felt like he wasn't connecting with his children; he couldn't relate to them. He had nothing to brag about. His inferiority complex kicked in. He concluded he was an inadequate father. Then Josey predicted he'd be a poor father. He thought she already knew he was a failing father. He reacted by swearing he would be a good father, and he meant it.

Frank had adopted his father's concept of a good father—a husband must manage his own family well and see that *his children obey him with proper respect* (1 Timothy 3:4–5). It was one he felt certain he could meet. Be a good provider. There'd always be food and clothing. He'd pay for his children's education and raise them to be obedient. When Kathy or Jill didn't live up to his expectations, Frank became frustrated. Like his father, Frank resorted to punishment, to fear. To impress his fellow workers, he became a fun-loving party animal, but his inebriated behavior prevented him from developing close relationships with them. After a while, Frank's drinking became a habit, a habit that led to ugly behavior.

"Father argued that the money he spent on drinking had no effect on the budget for the family. On normal days, Father returned home for dinner and talked to us about our interests and our friends. Then one day, his fragile father self-image took a hit. Remember the first school play you asked us all to attend?"

Jill nods.

"Well, Father encouraged many of his friends at work to come. He said you were in the play. He failed to realize that you *worked in* the play. You were a set designer. His friends later asked which character you were. He had to admit he was wrong. You weren't an actor. He felt so embarrassed. Mom said it took a long time after that before he asked about your school involvements. Later, she learned he'd been teased about how little he knew about his children."

"So, you're saying Mom felt sorry for Father?"

"More than that. I think she tried to get him to overlook the mistakes, to see that he was a good father. She pointed out that we were hardworking like he was. We had high marks at school. We were well dressed, respectful, orderly. I think she tried to build up his image of a good father in ways that he would appreciate. Mom said that is what you do for the people you love."

"So Mom loved him." Jill shook her head. The man her mother painted was so different from what she thought he was.

"Mom loved her man, a vulnerable man."

Thinking that Jill doesn't hear her last comment, Kathy reaches out and touches Jill's hand. When Jill adjusts her attention, Kathy continues.

"Early in Mom's hospital stay when it was clear that her illness was terminal, Josey purchased a plot for Mom. When Mom left Frank, she had very little money. Josey also ordered a headstone for Mom and let Mom prepare the inscription. Then Mom asked me to purchase the plot next to hers for Father. She said she wanted Father to know that when he died, he could still be close to her. The fact that he phoned her almost every day when she left him and came to the hospital every day told her that he would be very lonely when she died. The words on the headstone were for him. She wanted him to remember her feelings for him but also feelings she wanted him to apply toward you and me."

"Like she's talking to him from the grave."

"Exactly."

"What made Mom think he would come to her grave?"

"He brought flowers to his mother's grave every year after she died. And Mom was right. In the beginning, Father came twice a week to Mom's grave. At least that's what the groundskeeper told me."

"You kept track of him after Mom died?"

"I thought I would. When we were in the hospital, he asked me to forgive him. Of course, I did. He promised to keep in touch. After the funeral, he disappeared. I checked at the GM plant where he worked and learned that he was fired. He'd been drinking heavily. New people were living in our old house. I couldn't find him, so I gave up. Then a little over a year later, before Christmas, he phoned me. Asked if I would meet him at the McDonald's. He insisted I come alone. I did."

Kathy looks down at the ground. Her head shakes ever so slightly. Finally, Jill asks what's wrong. Kathy takes a deep breath and continues her story, only now her voice drops to a whisper.

"He looked terrible." She checks for Jill's reaction. "He was clean and shaved, but his clothes hung so loose. His face was so thin. When I asked if I could buy him a coffee and a burger, he agreed. It went down so fast I offered to buy a second one. He declined. He asked how things were going with me, with Joyce, and with Larry. When I asked how he was doing, all I got were vague answers. He moved to some basement suite. He worked here and there. I think my questions prompted him to leave. He stood up, we hugged, he thanked me for coming, and then he left."

"Didn't you try to follow him?"

"No. That's what Larry asked too. His departure was so unexpected. I stood there shocked. I thought we finally reestablished contact, and then he was gone."

"Did he ever call again?"

"The following year, about the same time. He looked just as bad as the year before. He wore the same clothes too. This time, after talking about my family, he was a little more forthcoming about his situation. He didn't say so, but I could tell he was lonely. He assured me he was still living in the same basement suite. He almost got kicked out because of his drinking. To solve the problem, he doesn't return to his place when he's drunk."

"You said you thought he was lonely. What made you think so?"

"Right after we hugged, he said no one cares about him. I was the only one who even knew he was alive or cared. He claimed even God deserted him. He thanked me for coming again and then left. I thought of trying to follow him. But I decided against it. If I tried to follow him, he might not call again."

Kathy continued describing the development of her relationship with her father over the next decade. When Frank came to visit her the third time in the beginning of December, Kathy convinced him to meet her seven-month-old son, Jack, and four-and-half-year-old daughter, Joyce. At that time, he fabricated a story about dropping into Markham to pick up supplies for the company he worked for. He claimed he volunteered to do the pickup so he could see his daughter and his grandchild. Kathy suspected the story was meant more for her than her children.

Frank enjoyed seeing the children. The following year, he looked forward to Kathy bringing her children to McDonald's. She did. After two years of meeting together, he inquired as to the birth dates of Joyce and Jack. The following April, he showed up the day before Jack's third birthday at McDonald's. He brought a card and little gift, and for the first time, he wore a different shirt and slacks. He did the same for Joyce's seventh birthday in June. Kathy's first attempt to encourage Frank to meet Larry failed. It took two more years of birthday-appearance coaxing for Frank to agree to show up at Joyce's ninth birthday party. Even then he first confirmed that Josey would not be there. He met Larry, felt accepted, and agreed to join them for Christmas dinner.

Frank initiated the next elements of family bonding. It started mid-afternoon with Frank shopping for a couple of bran muffins for his lunch. Unexpectedly, he met two elderly women from the church he and Alice used to go to. He was unshaved, in greasy, torn jeans, and wearing an old flannel shirt. A frayed hole in his right runner showed he had let himself go. He feared if the gray-haired busybodies confirmed his identity, word would get back to Josey about how scruffy he looked. Frank's attempt to escape froze when one of the women loudly called his name. A glance at the customers in the aisle left no doubt. He was in the spotlight. Feeling like a thief caught in the act of shoplifting, he turned around and faked a friendly greeting.

To his amazement, the ladies recognized him from Alice's funeral. They shook his hand, sympathized with him over his loss, and inquired about how he was doing. After his often-repeated vague answers about work, he claimed he was picking up some muffins for break time. Then they asked about Kathy. Tension drained. Specific information about his daughter, his grandchildren, and their recent birthday parties transformed him into feeling like a real father. The older woman, Bertha, asked about Kathy's birthday. Frank couldn't remember. Often, when he brought a birthday card for Jack or Joyce, he wished he could remember when Kathy was born. He was too embarrassed to ask. In his mind, it confirmed what a poor father he was. His silence enabled Bertha's friend, while thinking out loud, to list birthdays of her friends.

"October," she announced confidently.

"Yes," chimed Frank. "October 19." He knew the number, but the month had escaped him.

True to his previous pattern, he called Kathy up the day before her birthday to meet at their usual place. He surprised her with a card, and she surprised him with an invitation to join her for dinner the next day to celebrate her birthday. Even though he was wearing his best clothes, he excused himself, saying he wasn't dressed to go out. He was dropping in to see her while doing a company errand. By this time, he expected that Kathy didn't believe his story about work bringing him to Markham, but she let him use it, so he did. On the spot, Kathy changed plans. She said the family was going out to the Swiss Chalet and what he was wearing was fine. All he had to do was stay overnight. He agreed. That was the first time he stayed at her place overnight. The success of that bold move enabled him later to ask about the date of Larry's birthday. For Larry's next birthday, Frank repeated the pattern with which he had become comfortable.

As Jill listens to Kathy's story about what seemed like a fictitious father, she begins to understand how Kathy's opinion about her father might have changed. She thinks that twenty years of her father visiting on their birthdays and for Christmas could earn him a new respect. One thing bothers Jill about her father's life.

"Did he ever ask about me?"

"No. And I had no idea if you were alive or not. I only found out that you were still living when Julie visited Josey."

After Jill's nod, Kathy continues, "Then last year, in late October, I received a phone call from Mrs. Shadha. She asked if I knew Frank Rezley. She told me she was his landlady. Then I heard Father died."

Instantly, Kathy begins crying, as if she just received the news. Jill holds her sister. She concludes that Kathy loved her father, a situation Jill admits she cannot relate to.

As Kathy regains control, she explains, "I thought something was wrong. Last Christmas, his clothes looked unwashed. He looked thinner than usual. When I asked him if I could take him to a doctor, he refused. Then he didn't come for Joyce's birthday or Jack's. I got real worried, asked questions, but learned nothing. Then he missed my birthday. I thought he was avoiding me because I pushed too hard for him to see a doctor. A week later, Mrs. Shadha phoned. Now I wish I'd have insisted he see a doctor."

Kathy bursts into tears again. While Jill holds her sister, she looks at the headstone of her parents. Pieces of the inscription return to her. "*Keeps no record of wrongs, always protects, always hopes.*" Jill feels the message is meant as much for her as her father.

As Kathy regains her composure, she tells Jill she needs to stop at home to freshen up. Jill offers to phone and ask Bill to drive her back to the hotel, but Kathy declines. She explains that her husband is working late and her children are out. She really needs the company of others to take her out of her present mood. Driving Jill back to her hotel is a perfect way to distract her.

On the drive to the hotel, Kathy tells Jill what she learned from Mrs. Shadha a week after her father's funeral. Frank began lodging with Mr. and Mrs. Shadha almost two years after he sold his house. Because of his drinking, he couldn't stay in any place for very long. In desperation, he turned to the minister in his church. An appeal to the members brought forth a leery Mr. and Mrs. Shadha. They accepted Frank on two conditions: if his drinking interfered with their life, he was out, no second chance. The second condition was, after signing a contract, he arranged with his bank that they were the only ones who could draw on his account and only for the specified rent. Mrs. Shadha admitted when they took Frank in, they were in need of extra money. If they weren't, they wouldn't have accepted him.

Frank made a point of not coming to the suite drunk. At times, it meant staying at a hostel or sleeping in the park. For spending money, Frank worked on neighbors' and friends' vehicles. As his odd jobs dwindled, he began turning in recyclables. Six months before he died, he ran out of money for rent. Since he was no trouble, the Shadhas let him stay. They knew in the end, all he had was his tools and some money for food. After hearing no sound of activity downstairs for a couple of days, Mrs. Shadha investigated. She found Frank resting peacefully with a picture of Kathy's family on his chest. Kathy's phone number and the family's birth dates were penned on the back.

Kathy accepts Bill's offer to join Jill and him for dinner at the hotel. The early part of the evening slides by quickly. Bill engages Kathy with his probing questions about her family. After the dinner, Jill entertains them with stories and pictures from Daniel's album. Jill's two unopened family albums prompt an invitation for Bill and Jill to visit Sunday. Kathy promises to see if she can round up her children for some portion of the day, and Jill volunteers to see if Josey will come.

When Kathy leaves to drive home, Bill looks forward to spending some time with Jill. She dashes his hopes by turning in early. The stories about her father need reviewing. Perhaps a flaw can be found, a flaw that would cast a shadow on the image that her father really was a caring man. Jill's departing somber demeanor puzzles Bill. Anger or frustration after Jill hears about her father from Kathy is what he expects. He returns to the restaurant, orders a glass of white wine, and sits in a corner, sipping it, wishing Jill was beside him or that they were strolling through the park on the other side of the street.

JILL'S CONFESSION

NINE O'CLOCK THE NEXT morning, Jill and Bill drive to Brampton. They expect to meet with the property manager by midmorning. Excitement marks Jill's outlook for the day. She spills memories of the two-story brick house; the rooms; the balcony; the dolphin wind chimes; the long, curved driveway with a hedge of yellow roses lining one side; the flowers by the back patio; and their fragrances. Pointing to the back seat, Jill says she brought Josey's album so she could name the flowers, if they're still there. Without any encouragement from Bill, her stories turn to the adventures with the Creative Arts Society of Brampton at the Brick Theater. She wishes she could once again meet Karen Parkelle and Linda Bryce, the bank employees who shared the rent of Josey's place.

Bill enjoys the sound of Jill's memories. They pour out of her like water trickling down the stream. It's a joy he hears too rarely from her. He waits until the descriptions exhaust her.

"I hope you won't be disappointed."

Jill looks at him for an explanation.

"Things will have changed."

"Oh, I know some of the flowers won't be there—"

"Or the dolphin wind chimes." Bill recalls that is what Jill described to Amber when Jill talked about her grandmother's house in Brampton. The chimes Jill described the first time were from the Chicago restaurant balcony. Bill concludes both images were a time of comfort for Jill. He's pleased he was a part of one of those times.

"Or the wind chimes," agrees Jill with a chuckle. "But going back and seeing the place is like going back to a, a—"

"A moment of heaven," adds Bill.

"Exactly! That is exactly what I thought of it when I was there."

Listening to Jill's excitement, he knows her time in Brampton was very special. Judging by her tone, he surmises this place is as important to her as Josey. At the same time, he suspects something awfully dire forced her to leave, something that she hasn't revealed to him. He wonders how important it is now. He chooses not to spoil her moment of joy.

When they introduce themselves to the property manager, Bill notes Marvin's nervousness. Once the manager confirms that they're really there to consider the suggested improvements and not to buy the property, his anxiety disappears. Josey's lawyer's phone call the other day to check on the financial state of the property had him concerned. Marvin briefs them on the proposed projects and presents two estimates for each of the projects and his recommendations. Bill thanks him for his thorough work, takes the folder with his documents, and follows Marvin to Josey's house.

The moment they reach the driveway, Jill instructs Bill to adopt a turtle pace. As they crawl toward the house, she soaks in the scene, the changes, but says nothing.

As Marvin tours them through the house, Bill whispers in Jill's ear, "Remember, we aren't buying the house." Bill holds up the folder of Marvin's recommendations. His comment still puzzles her. "You look so disappointed, like you're trying to drive down the price of the property."

She responds with a gentle swat. As they continue their walk-through, Bill evaluates the proposed changes. Jill lounges in the memories of the summer she spent here. When they go out for lunch, Jill admits she'll second anything that Bill says about Marvin's recommendations.

When Bill asks her for her opinion of the property, she focuses on the deterioration of the grounds. "I'm glad Josey isn't here to see it," she begins. "She so loved the gardens. Now it seems like the property has lost its richness, its appeal." Almost all the tenants' requests dealt with some aspect of upgrading the house.

"If you were to move in here, would you ask for the same changes?" inquires Bill.

"Oh yes. But so much more needs to be done." Jill places her grandmother's album on the table and opens it. "Just look at this." She flips page after page. She points to a picture of the yellow rose hedge. "It was this landscaping that lured Josey and my grandfather into even looking at the house. With work, we could restore it. Don't you think?"

Bill catches Jill's pronoun, "we" but chooses to deal with the implication of living in Brampton. "I have my garden in Camrose."

Jill misses a note of concern in Bill's voice. "Is one garden much different than another?"

"Mine is. My snapdragon is the young guy upgrading his science mark so he can register for the pipefitting course. My rose is the single mother on her last year of training to be a hairdresser. My chess-playing teen is an ivy geranium needing fertilizer to bloom."

As Bill lists clients from the Wellness Center, Jill recognizes stories that Bill has shared with her before.

"I look forward to seeing them succeed. It's like helping a kid learn how to ride a bike. Once they get the hang of their particular skill, they soar like a bird. At that point, I feel like I'm flying with them. Those are my flowers. Their successes are my flowers' blossoms."

"Sounds like you're tending the Lord's garden. He blessed you with the skill of empathizing and helping, and you are using that talent to care for his people. I understand." Jill closes her album and stands up. "Ready to go?"

Dropping the money for the lunch on the table, Bill hurries after Jill. "You're not disappointed, are you?"

As they walk out of the restaurant, Jill answers, "Helping people is your passion, like Amber's is painting or Joseph's was gardening. It's a blessing when you can chase your passion."

"Or yours is stage setting."

"Yes, it is."

When Bill opens the front car door for Jill, he is still uncertain if she is upset with him for desiring to live in Camrose. Jill surprises him with an affectionate kiss. Then flashing a playful smile, she drops to her seat and closes the door. Bill begins his drive back to Oshawa, feeling content. Leaving his home isn't an option he wants to consider. He works his way into highway traffic.

Jill's thoughts turn to the last time she left Brampton. Then she was running from Josey. Today, she is going to see Josey. Before, she left alone, sad. Now, she is leaving with Bill, content. *Life's so good.*

Dave creeps into her memories, the major reason for her departure years ago. While she hasn't heard or seen a hint of Dave, she worries that somehow she will end up running into him. To her, he means unfinished business, business that needs tending to, but business she wants to avoid if she can help it. She reviews her remaining holiday itinerary. Three days and then she flies home. She tells herself she has nothing to worry about.

"You're sure quiet. Problems?"

Jill looks at the silent radio. Bill often drives with the radio off. On the way to Brampton, the silence gave Jill a chance to talk about her grandmother's house and all the things she looked forward to seeing. Now it showed that her mind was elsewhere.

"Kind of." Her response slips out naturally. She wishes it hadn't.

"About your grandmother's place?"

Jill worries that any talk about Josey's place could lead to why she left it long ago. "Not really."

"Something you feel comfortable sharing?"

Jill hates to be dishonest. Bill could easily take it as a sign that she still doesn't trust him. After she catches Bill glancing at her for the second time, waiting for a response, she decides to discuss the issue that sent her to her room early last night.

"It's about my father, or rather about Kathy's view of my father." Jill summarizes Kathy's description of the experiences she had with her father after her mother's funeral. "Listening to her, I get the feeling that he was a misunderstood, lost man. He needed help."

"And you feel guilty for not being around to do anything for him?"

"No. Kathy's image of him is so unreal. It's not what she used to think of him. He was a mean, loudmouth bully. It's why Kathy ran away. It's why I left home."

"Could it be that he changed after the death of your mother?"

"At first, I thought so. At least I wanted to think so. But Kathy seems to have come to the same conclusion as my mother." Jill can't say her father had an inferiority complex. She promised. But to her, Kathy has a false impression. "He was a needy man."

"Do you think Kathy misread your father?"

"That's the problem. From all the things she described he did, I can't fault her for her changed view of him."

"So you can't reconcile your vision of your father with that of your mother and Kathy?"

"Yes. It feels horrible. It's like I'm missing an important landmark. Not seeing a particular sign or building or park that tells you where you are. It's gone."

"Sort of like the captains a long time ago determining their course by the North Star. Now that you can't see that star, you feel lost."

"Exactly. Now I'm confused. I can't help question whether I have a clear grasp of reality. Can I even count on myself for anything?"

"If you think Kathy's experiences are based on fact, can you accept her impression of your father?"

"I don't know if I want to."

"And deny truth?"

"I don't know if I can accept that truth."

"Maybe that is something you need to pray about." Bill glances at Jill for her reaction.

"And that's another thing I can't appreciate." Irritation raises Jill's voice. She shifts around in her seat, facing Bill, ready to see his reaction as well as hear his words. Now is the time to challenge him.

"Praying?"

"Yes." Jill's response is swift, as if she's blocking a blow and preparing a counterattack. "Every time I hear you pray, do you know how you start? You begin with Dear *Father*. Do you have any idea what that does to me?" Jill's challenge shoots out like a machine gun spitting bullets. "It immediately turns me off."

Bill looks at Jill to determine if he has heard correctly.

"Do you know what *Father* means to me? It means a hard, uncaring, mean, violent man. It means look out. He's the one who's about to punish you, fairly or not. Asking for anything can result in his wrath. So why would I dare ask for anything? Why would I dare hope to get a favorable answer? I've learned I have no one I can count on except myself. No one."

Jill's breathing comes in gulps. Her red face stares intently at Bill. Silence greets her outburst.

As Jill watches Bill driving, she is certain she has shocked him. She expects she has lost a friend and prepares to accept the consequences. When he signals, pulls over to the shoulder, and stops, she wonders if he'll get out of the car and leave her alone.

"Well?" she demands as he shifts to park. She wants a response from him before he leaves. It's the least he can do now that she has shown him who she really is.

Jill stares at Bill's every motion. When he turns the engine off, she takes a deep breath. *He* is *about to walk out.* She thinks of Joseph and how he left her, all of a sudden, out of the blue. He unbuckles his seat belt. *Oh, why couldn't have I kept my mouth shut?*

Bill turns and faces Jill. "I'm so sorry. I had no idea my father reference has such a negative connotation."

"Well, it does. And now you can see why Kathy's version of my father grates me. It can't be true. And even if it is, it can't be for me."

Bill looks at Jill and struggles with a response.

She searches for a sign of rejection.

When Bill begins to speak, his words come slowly but with a conviction that he has heard everything she said. "Jill, there's so much I would like to pose for you." He pauses, trying to choose what he most wants her to consider first. "I'd like to address your need for landmarks. Okay?"

Jill has no idea where Bill intends to lead her, but she nods, trusting that a challenge is coming.

"When you pray, can you call on God instead of Father?"

"I can, but it makes no difference. God is an impersonal being. He doesn't care about me. When you asked me to pray about coming to Ontario, I did. I prayed to God. He didn't hear me. He didn't answer me. I don't know how you can say you have a personal relationship with him. It sounds phony."

Jill's words give Bill more reason to pause. "Have you addressed your prayers to Jesus?"

"What difference would that make?"

"Do you believe he died?"

"Yes."

"So we can be forgiven and go to heaven?"

"Yes."

"Doesn't that sound like *he* is loving, *he* is caring?"

Jill catches Bill's emphasis on *he*. She crosses her arms in front, feeling exposed. Guessing that Bill has figured out that she doesn't trust males in general is more than she intends to reveal. Bill's eyes focus on her. Remembering his question, she nods.

"So you could pray to Jesus?"

"When you have done things a certain way for so long, it's not easy."

"I know, but I also know that you can change."

"You're just being nice."

"I'd like to think I'm being more than nice. My confidence in your ability to change is based on facts and your genes." Bill smiles as he sees Jill's puzzled look. She isn't into challenging him. She's trying to understand him.

"I think if you ask Daniel, he would say it is very hard to change something that you have believed in all your life. When you and Joseph separated, Daniel told me he had absolutely no doubt that you were the cause. You were so self-centered. Daniel claimed you always were. And yet when you apologized to him, when you showed you were concerned for his feelings, he changed. Daniel saw change in you, and he changed. You both have the ability to get over long-held views. And that's how I know you can get over the effect your father has on you. Does that help?"

"It sounds encouraging."

"And if you remember, that is something we prayed for together. Don't you think Daniel's change was one of God's blessings?"

"Don't you want to give me credit for choosing to apologize or credit to Daniel for accepting it?" A touch of irritation taints Jill's response.

"Certainly, you deserve credit for taking action. But where do you give credit for the confidence and the courage to carry out an action that you found very hard? And don't tell me that saying that you were wrong to Daniel was easy. Earlier, you said that God doesn't listen to you, doesn't respond to your prayers. I believe you said *he didn't answer me*. Perhaps what you need is a second set of eyes to help you see things more clearly. Maybe that's why you don't feel confident that you have a clear grasp of reality."

"And who would you suggest should be my second set of eyes?" Irritation returns to Jill's voice.

"For developing a clearer picture of the kind of person your mother was, perhaps your grandmother, and for your father, perhaps Kathy."

"And what about you? Are you a candidate to be a second set of eyes for me?"

"Only if you trust me."

Wanting to put an end to their conversation, Jill returns to her former seating position. When a vehicle passes by them, she says, "Maybe we should leave before someone pulls over to ask if we have car troubles."

When they return to Oshawa, Jill intends to go to her room to change from her traveling clothes. Josey had invited them to join her for supper at a restaurant owned by one of her friends. Jill wants to impress Josey's friends. Before Jill enters the elevator to go to her room, she promises to meet Bill in the lobby as soon as she's ready.

Bill sits by the pool in the sun, reviewing the documents in Marvin's folder. Satisfied that he can't detect any concerns, he browses through the daily paper that someone left on an adjacent table. By the time he checks his watch for the third time, he wonders why Jill is taking so long. He suspects something might be wrong and debates phoning from the front desk. He crosses the lobby in time to see Jill step out of the elevator, radiating energy. He looks twice.

Jill is dressed in a pale-green outfit, one that he's seen her wear to church. A light-green scarf with waves of orange loosely wraps around her neck. Her hair is fluffed and tucked neatly behind her ears. For the first time since they arrived in Oshawa, she's wearing earrings and lipstick. It is also the first time he's seen her take her small black purse or wear her black high-heeled shoes. The clerk at the front desk gives a low whistle of approval. In response, Jill spins around.

Seeing tongue-tied Bill, she says, "Can't a girl get dressed up once in a while?"

"Definitely! But—" He waves his hand, directing her to turn around again. When she is finished, he glances at his clothes, sandals, jeans, and T-shirt. Realizing the place they are going to eat must be a classy one, he says, "I have to change."

As Bill starts to hurry to the elevator, Jill asks for the folder, which he is carrying. He hands it to her and rushes off. After the elevator button is pressed, frustration darkens his face. *She couldn't have told me to change earlier?*

As Bill hopes, the evening meal is an informal affair. The casual apparel of Tony and Faye Martoni sets Bill's mind at ease. He guesses Jill's reason for dressing up had something to do with Josey's intent to proudly display her found granddaughter. At one point in the evening meal, Bill thinks about the parable of the prodigal son. Listening to the praise Josey heaps on her granddaughter makes him think of the father celebrating the return of his prodigal son. The comparison pulls a smile from Bill.

Talk of Mr. Martoni's small chain of restaurants and his dream of expanding to Brampton with the help of Josey catches Bill's attention. He wonders if Tony's many questions about Jill's work experiences in Mary and Ed's bakery is an interview for a management position in his restaurant. Had Josey suggested that Jill dress up to impress the restaurateur? The possibility that Josey is preparing to tempt Jill into moving back to Ontario concerns him. Certainly, the timing of this get-together, after Jill returns from Brampton, seems ideal. At the end of the evening, as they part company with the Martonis, Bill forces himself to believe that this was a harmless social event.

After Bill drives Josey to McKenzie Manor, she invites them up for tea. Jill glances at her watch. While it's only nine in the evening and early for her, Jill thinks it would be late for her grandmother. Josey's urging succeeds in convincing them to come up to her room.

While making the tea, Josey fills the time by discussing her friends and their ambitions. With the tea poured, she changes topics. "So tell me, what do you think of the grand old place," says Josey, referring to her house in Brampton. She passes the sugar to Bill.

"I loved it," says Jill, full of passion. "It brings back so many wonderful memories. I could have stayed there all day."

Together, Josey and Jill review many highlights of the summer Jill spent there.

For a while, Josey gets lost in telling stories about the times she and her husband lived there. Then, as if she is reminded of the main purpose of calling them to her room, she says, "It will be so hard to give it up. I know someday I'll have to face that. Just like I have to face dealing with its upkeep. Why don't you tell me what you learned while I'm still in love with the place and willing to spend some money?"

Jill looks to Bill for his thoughts. He endorses each recommendations made by Marvin, explaining why he agrees that they are needed.

Josey looks to Jill. "And if you were to move into my place again, would you want all these things done too?" She points to the folder that Bill closes.

"Those and more," confesses Jill. She describes the conditions of the yard and what she thinks should be done to bring it back to its former beauty.

After listening for fifteen minutes to Jill's landscaping dreams, Josey says, "That's what I like to hear, someone who loves the place as much as I do. You know, for one hundred dollars, I could turn it over to you. I know you'll take good care of it. George would like that."

"Oh no." Jill and Bill both respond at the same time.

"That place is way too valuable," says Jill.

"The location itself means a parcel like that would sell for, I guess, at least one million dollars, maybe more. I confess I haven't studied market values here, but it's worth a fortune."

"Then I guess I should approve Marvin's suggestions. He'll be glad to hear you two agree with him. I have been putting these changes off for more than a year. I'll call him tomorrow morning. That's Saturday, right?"

Jill nods.

"I'm sure he'll be glad to get to work on them."

Before they leave, Josey confirms that Bill and Jill will bring her to church. She also asks that the Sunday visit to Kathy's be reduced to going for supper. She admits she tires more recently. "An afternoon nap will carry me through the evening. That's what I did today."

Half an hour later, they walk to the elevator. Josey makes one last request. "Jill, would you bring your family albums tomorrow morning? I know you're bringing them to Kathy's, but it will be easier for me to look at them here." Looking at Bill's disappointed face, Josey promises that he can have Jill back for the rest of the day.

On the drive back to the hotel, Jill launches into the landscaping changes she brought up with Josey. She notes Bill made no comments while they were at her grandmother's. Thinking he has some concerns, she asks his advice on her little projects.

As they pull up to their hotel, Bill changes the topic. "About tomorrow—"

"Oh, I'm so looking forward to showing Josey my albums! You know, we only have three days left here." Before Bill can say anything else, she adds, "I know Josey will hear the same stories when I show Kathy the albums Sunday night. I think she just wants to spend a little more time with me."

"I'm sure she enjoys hearing you talk about your family. She hasn't had much of a chance to know them."

Bill also realizes that Jill may be more right than she realizes. He suspects her grandmother wants to ask some fairly personal questions. When Josey met with him, she surprised him with the questions she posed about Jill's emotional health and about Joseph and their marriage. Bill couldn't help wondering if Julie shared more information with Josey than she let on.

Jill remembers Josey's earlier observation of Bill's reaction. Looking at Bill, she adds, "I hope you don't mind that I'll be there tomorrow morning. I know we haven't spent much time together since we came here."

"I knew that the main reason for coming here is so you could spend time with your grandmother. Don't worry about it."

He agrees that they can relax by the pool in the afternoon and talk. There'd still be time enough to explore the park across the street from the hotel.

"You *are* wonderful," says Jill, overjoyed. "And I want you to know I *really* appreciate you driving to Brampton to see Josey's house."

They get out of the car and walk to the hotel.

"And not the drive back?" Bill smiles, remembering their roadside conversation.

"About that," says Jill. Her tone changes. She stops and faces him. Concern clouds her face. "You said a number of things that I have to try and work out. I thought about them while I was changing for tonight. It was too much for me. I'll consider them later this evening. If I have problems, I'll come and see you. Okay?"

He shoots a quick glance to the restaurant patio. Several patrons are relaxing with a drink, but tables for two are available. He anticipates enjoying a glass or two of wine with Jill. The dinner with the Martonis still bothers him.

In particular, he remembers Mr. Martoni expressing his gratitude for Josey agreeing to join him on investing in the Brampton expansion. Later, it occurred to Bill that Josey might be the one trying to attract Jill with a job, a management position, in an effort to convince her to move to Ontario. Such a position would be more exciting than being a receptionist in an insurance company, like she is now. And then there was Josey's request that Jill dress up for dinner. He wonders if Josey has talked to Jill about moving to Ontario.

"Depending upon when you call," he says. "I might be out there having some wine." He points to the patio, hoping she may join him.

Jill thanks him, checks the time that they will meet for breakfast, and heads for the elevator. Bill watches her step into the elevator and waves as the door closes. His attention turns to activity in the courtyard to his right. A small band is setting up for a function this evening. The desire for a glass of wine draws him to the patio. He enjoys the taste of the wine, but he misses Jill. His second-guessing the intentions of Tony Martoni and Josey leaves him frustrated.

When he enters his room, he checks the phone to see if Jill left a message. She didn't. He grabs the book he's been reading this trip, John Irving's *A Prayer for Owen Meany*, and drops into an armchair. The book serves its purpose. He doesn't realize the passing time until he rubs his eyes around midnight. Even the periodic, exuberant cheering and loud music from the courtyard don't distract him. Glancing at his watch, he concludes it's unlikely Jill will call. He goes to bed.

JOSEY'S SURPRISES

THE NEXT MORNING, JILL'S stories about her children fascinate Josey. When Jill closes the album, she isn't surprised to see how fast the morning has slipped away. What does surprise her is Josey's enthusiasm over Amber's paintings. Josey pleads for an opportunity to purchase one of Amber's works, saying she'll pay for the shipping and everything. As a temporary consolation, Jill gives Josey the photo of her family she took the day before Amber drove to Edmonton to live with Mary and Ed. Jill credits Bill for insisting on taking the picture. Holding the print close to her heart, Josey walks off to her bedroom. Jill suspects she is looking for a small frame.

Josey returns, holding a legal-sized folder. It's not the folder from Marvin. Her beaming face raises her granddaughter's curiosity. Josey shuffles to the table more slowly than normal. She sits down and places the folder midway between them.

"Jill, since your mother died, I've had the pleasure of spending a lot of time with Kathy and her family. I've been able to enjoy her children and help Kathy raise them. But you weren't around. I couldn't do anything for you."

"I'm sorry, Josey, but—"

Jill's grandmother shakes her head, cutting off Jill's excuse. "The loss has been mine, but it's also been yours too. I'm afraid you have no idea how much you've missed out. I hope with what I'm about to say to you, you will have an idea. You will also know that I have waited a long time to be able to do something for you to show how much I love you. First, I want to ask you if you are able to write a check to me for one hundred dollars."

"Yes, but what for?"

Josey opens the folder and hands Jill an offer-to-purchase form. "For my Brampton house, the one you love so much." Josey looks at her granddaughter as Jill struggles to find words.

Finally, Jill says, "You can't."

"Oh yes I can. My lawyer agrees I am of sound mind. I can do this." Josey smiles, knowing Jill thinks she's being too generous.

"That's not what I mean. You're too kind. And what is there for Kathy?"

"Never mind Kathy or her children. They are and have been well taken care of. I've had more than two decades to be there for them. Besides, Kathy knows what I am doing. She has no problem with it."

"But it's so valuable—"

"*You* are so valuable. And *you* love this place. I know you will take care of it. Rent it, or sell it. Do whatever you think is best for you and your family. At my age, I have no more use for such a large house or the money I get from it. All I do with my money is invest it with friends, like the Martonis or others. And I have done that. There's no need for me to do any more. But I haven't done anything for you. I would like this to be a start. Let me do this for you while I still can. Say yes and make *me* happy."

Tears flood Jill's eyes. "Yes. Yes." Jill rushes to her grandmother's opened arms. When Jill looks up, she sees Josey wiping her eyes too.

"Enough," says Josey, wanting to sweep away the emotional distraction. She has more matters to deal with. "Write your check for me and …" Josey opens the folder and points to sticky arrows, indicating where Jill needs to sign on the purchase agreement. "Let's make this legal. You'll notice possession is in December, on your birthday. Don't worry about taking care of the property. Marvin will take care of everything until you decide what you want to do with it."

"I can't believe it." Jill hands the signed papers to her grandmother.

"And I have a hard time believing I am able to finally do one of the things I thought I would never be able to do—see my other granddaughter so happy. When I look back over the years, I see three outstanding times in my life. The first is raising my children. I'm happy to see that you and I share that same joy. The second is enjoying my grandchildren. I fumbled there, but seeing you happy now kind of makes me feel a little better.

I know I've said this to you before, but it bears repeating. Keep a close connection with your grandchildren. You'll never regret it."

Jill nods and promises to do as she's instructed.

"And the other most important, most valuable part of my life was my marriage and then the retirement years with George and in particular the time we spent together in Brampton. Those times serve as a source of strength for me now."

Jill nods, remembering some stories that Josey told her while Jill spent the summer in Brampton.

Then somberness crosses Josey's face like a dark rain cloud. Before Jill can investigate what is bothering her grandmother, Josey softly asks, "You know I love you very much, and I wouldn't do anything to hurt you?" After Jill's acknowledgment, she continues, "I have to ask that, because at times in the past, I've been known to stick my nose in other people's business, particularly my family's."

Jill nods thinking of Josey criticizing her father's drinking and Josey bringing Dave to see her in Brampton.

"Now, I want to ask you some very personal questions. If you think it is too personal, then don't answer. I'll understand. But I also want you to know that I am trying to help."

Jill adjusts her position so that she is more firmly placed on the chair. Josey's expression reminds her of her mother sitting her down to explain something important.

"I am wondering how you would describe your feelings for Bill."

Josey leans forward, preparing to follow up on whatever answer Jill provides. Josey's preamble echoes in Jill's mind—"stick my nose in my family's business, wouldn't hurt you; I love you, too personal, don't answer." Jill's initial inclination is not to answer, but the words *wouldn't hurt you* and *I love you* overrule her reaction.

"He's a friend." Hearing her answer, Jill realizes her understatement. "A good friend."

"A good friend," repeats Josey, thinking out loud.

Jill nods in agreement.

As Jill relaxes in her chair, Josey says, "So, your good friend spent considerable time visiting you in the hospital?"

Jill nods.

"And he was there for you when you came out of the hospital and when you wanted to purchase a replacement vehicle?"

Jill nods again.

"I understand that the two of you have spent considerable time together since then." Jill's look of surprise prompts Josey to explain. "Julie."

Jill realizes that Josey knows a lot more about her than she thought.

"And then Bill accompanies you here even though he has no relatives in the area." Josey lets the last tidbit of information take root before she poses her question. "You don't suppose that Bill has very strong feelings for you, do you?"

Jill reviews her grandmother's analysis. *She's asking me if Bill loves me?* The presumed question scares her. The concept of love triggers the words on her mother's tombstone. She finds herself checking patient, kind, no record of wrongs, perseveres, trusts. Bill's done all of them. She looks up at her grandmother with the disturbing awareness—*He loves me!* One last word from the tombstone pinches Jill—*hopes.* Her mind races to Bill's words, "*Niagara Falls, Canada's honeymoon capital.*" Bill's intention becomes clear. *He hopes we'll get married while we are down here!*

"Jill?" Josey searches for a response.

Not wanting to concede that Josey is right, Jill says, "Possibly."

Recognizing her granddaughter's awakening revelation, Josey pokes for more information. "What is it about Bill that attracts you most?"

"Well, we both like gardening. He's always there to help me, support me."

"And wasn't it like that with your last husband?"

"It's more than that. I really enjoy being around Bill. He understands me, sometimes better than I do myself. He values what I say, like I know what I'm talking about. He's had university, and yet he still thinks I have something to offer."

"Does that mean if he wasn't around anymore that you would miss him?"

The question shocks Jill. *Bill, not around!* It never occurred to her. Without much hesitation, she says, "Yes." After the words escape from her mouth, she is surprised with her response.

"Have you ever let him in on that?"

Jill shakes her head.

"And why not? Don't you love him?"

Joseph's accusation pierces her.

"I don't know." She starts crying.

"Is there something about him that's a problem?"

"Something about me?" says Jill, sobbing. "Joseph said I was incapable of being loving."

"And he said that when you were splitting up?"

Jill nods. "He said I didn't love him."

"After twenty-five years!" When no response comes from Jill, Josey adds, "Perhaps in the end you were taking him for granted. Tell me. Does Bill agree with his assessment of you?"

She shakes her head. "Bill points to how I love my children. He says I am loving."

"I would tend to agree with him." Josey's answer is quick and confident, but it fails to reassure Jill. "So why would Joseph think you weren't loving?"

Jill remains silent.

"Jill?" Josey's voice is soft. Her hand lifts Jill's head until Jill is looking at her.

"I don't know."

Jill's lie is accepted. Josey stands up and signals Jill to do the same. In the comfort of her arms, Josey whispers, "Sweep that notion of you not being loving away like dirt tracked into the house."

While still in her grandmother's arms, Jill recalls a deep male voice saying, "*Fifty-fifty, fifty-fifty. I give your marriage a 50 percent chance of success.*" The meaning then was Joseph was the only loving partner in her marriage. Tormented by guilt, Jill whispers in a barely audible tone, "What if it was Joseph's love for me that carried our marriage for twenty-six years? What if our marriage failed because I did not love him? What if I don't know how to love a husband?"

As if sharing a secret, Josey whispers, "That's nonsense. All you have to do is find out what Bill is interested in or wants. Just like you did for your children. Then support him in it. Join him or help him. Do you think I was interested in gardening when George retired?"

Jill pulls away from her grandmother to see if she is serious.

"No. But I worked with him in it. After a time, I liked it. I think I liked it because I was with him, but the thing is what I liked most is he was happy. Are you going to tell me you can't do that with Bill?"

"No," Jill mutters. She thinks about what Bill would like. *Niagara Falls. Impossible. Tomorrow we go to Markham to visit Kathy. Tuesday we fly home. There's not enough time.*

Josey's voice cuts into her scrutinizing. "You know, Bill and I had a good conversation. I can tell you I think he is a good man. If you think he is right for you and you want to prevent him from slipping through your fingers, you should let him know how you really feel." To counter Jill's blank stare, Josey nods a reassurance.

I can't. Ashamed of ignoring Bill's only wish for coming to Ontario, Jill once again seeks the comfort of her grandmother's arms. *I've only thought of what I wanted when we came here. How can Bill possibly want to marry such a selfish person?*

"My goodness! Look at the time!" The alarm in Josey's voice pulls Jill out of her self-imposed misery. "I promised Bill you'd be back for lunch. Why don't you call him? If he hasn't eaten yet, tell him you are on your way."

Without thinking of questioning her grandmother, Jill does as she is instructed. Jill calls Bill's room. No answer. She leaves a message. Calling the front desk works. The clerk sees Bill tanning by the pool. He promises to give him Jill's message.

"I have a great idea," says Josey, a little excited. "Why don't you and Bill have a quiet, romantic dinner at the hotel tonight? The hotel has a private dining room. It's actually designed for eight, but I'm sure I can get it for you tonight."

"It's Saturday night! At this late time, you'll never get it." The prospect excites Jill because she knows Bill would love that time together.

"Leave it to me." Josey takes the phone from Jill. When her call goes through, Josey gives her name and asks for Gerald. He's the manager. Jill's reservation is secure. "My treat," says Josey.

"How—"

"How am I able to do that?" interprets Josey with a big smile. "A couple of years ago, I hired him." Seeing Jill's puzzled look, Josey adds, "Did I forget to tell you I'm part owner of the hotel?"

Jill's jaw drops.

"Go. Go now and make Bill's day." After a moment, she adds, "And night."

Following her grandmother's direction, Jill meets Bill in the hotel cafeteria. Wanting a light lunch, Jill orders a chicken salad. Bill settles for barbecue wings. During their lunch, Jill first shares the news of Josey's gift of a "romantic" dinner for two in the private room. When Bill suggests they start the afternoon by tanning at the pool, Jill returns to her room and changes to her bathing suit. Navy shorts and a light-blue, cheesecloth low-back tank top serve as her public cover. After a couple of hours, the pool area feels like an oven. They retreat to the shade of the trees in the park across the street. Wandering through some of the park's many paths reminds them of their Sunday evening walks in Camrose.

During their walk in the park, Jill tells Bill that Josey sold the house to her for one hundred dollars. She expects Bill's disbelief. His muted joy surprises her. After Bill agrees that using Marvin's services would be a good option for Jill, he turns silent. It takes several attempts at highlighting the park's natural beauty before Jill succeeds in engaging Bill in appreciating the park's assets.

Ten minutes before their dinner reservation, Jill knocks on Bill's door. When he answers, Jill smiles her approval. Bill wears his pressed green slacks and his loose-fitting Banff golf shirt. The white silk fabric with green collar, waist, and sleeve trim suggests richness.

Bill stands in awe of his dinner date. *What a difference an hour can make.* He looks down at her navy A-skirt, clinging low on her hips. Multicolored forms chaotically dart in every direction. Continuing his downward gaze, he recognizes her white-strapped sandals. Bill's eyes snap back to Jill's sleeveless short white shirt. The top three buttons are undone. The bottom of her shirt hangs a good two inches above the waist of her skirt. Afraid he'll be caught staring, he turns his attention to her hair. Her bangs bounce as her head moves. The rest of her hair is tucked neatly behind her ears except for a dozen strands that cling together and play with her right cheek.

"Our dining room is on the west side of the building. I thought it would still be very warm."

Bill knows Jill's caught him looking at her breasts. He quickly closes his door, checks to confirm it's locked, and then wraps his arm around

Jill's waist. Together, they walk to the elevator. He notices Jill's perfume. It's only the second time she has worn it on this trip.

From the moment they enter the elevated private room, they feel like honored guests. Their four-course menu awaits them. Shortly after the waiter takes their orders, the wine is poured. Appetizers follow. The number of selections makes it seem like they are at a buffet. Their salad's arrival distracts them from the delay for their entrées. After their dessert, their server opens large glass doors and invites them to enjoy their third glass of wine on the balcony. Jill and Bill glance at each other, smiling. The same thought enters each of their minds—Family Conference in Chicago. While they are sipping their wine, Jill lets slip that her view of the park from her bedroom is better.

"I thought your room is two doors down from mine, overlooking the courtyard."

"It was," confesses Jill. "Until last night. Didn't the noise bother you?"

"I heard it, but I guess I tuned it out."

"I couldn't think. Couldn't sleep. I phoned the front desk. The conditions I stressed when booking is that I had to have a no smoking room and a quiet room. All the night manager could offer me was a small room on the sixth floor, facing the park. I took it. I packed everything and moved up last night. It was so dark I really didn't know what view I had until this morning. My balcony's much smaller than this one, but there is room for two chairs and a little stand. Want to come up and see it?"

After indulging in one more glass of wine, they go to Jill's room.

As soon as Jill enters her room, she slips her sandals off, complaining they are not broken in yet. As Jill works her way down the right side of her bed, a narrow passageway leading to the balcony door, Bill examines the narrow room. The washroom is on his left. A narrow footpath leads to a nightstand and a closet.

"You coming?" Jill stands before the opening to her balcony.

Bill kicks off his shoes and follows. For a while, they lean on the rail and examine the park from above. The Saturday night traffic and the commercial district off to their right hold their attention. When the heat reflecting off the building begins to stifle them, Jill leads the way back into her room. Bill follows, sliding the glass door closed.

"Did you secure the door?" asks Jill, a little concerned as she stands near the end of her bed.

Bill looks by the door but can't find the lock button to press.

"Don't worry about. I'll take care of it," she says as she starts toward Bill.

They near each other and turn to step sideways. Jill takes a deep breath to squeeze by Bill. Pressure against the wall retards her progress more than she expects. Then she realizes Bill is leaning into her instead of away.

She looks up to see a grinning face. Uncertain if he really means to trap her against the wall, she presses against him to get by. He matches her pressure, forcing her back against the wall while he chuckles with delight. His hands rest against the wall, blocking escape to the right or left.

"Yes?" She guesses what Bill is planning now that he is alone in her room.

"Remember when we were leaving Brampton, when we were standing by the car, when you thanked me for driving to see your grandmother's place?"

"Yes."

"You thanked me for a good day."

Jill remembers planting a quick kiss on Bill's surprised lips.

"Well, I would like to thank you for a wonderful afternoon and evening."

Jill slides her arms up and around Bill. She draws him even closer. Neither hurries to end their embrace. When they separate, Jill says, "I guess you really did appreciate our time together."

"I did."

With her arms still around Bill's neck, she adds, "It's my turn to thank you."

"For?"

"For coming to Oshawa and being so patient while I've been meeting with my family."

Their lips meet. Jill pulls herself even tighter against Bill. As she stretches their embrace, she feels Bill's hands ascending on her bare back, tentatively exploring. She tilts her head back slightly and is pressed more firmly against the wall.

In a soft voice, she says, "You really do want me, don't you?"

The answer is a whisper, as if only she should hear it. "In any and every way I can, now and forever." His hands continue to probe new territory.

"Are you sure? You know, I can be a real pain."

Bill bends back and looks into Jill's eyes. "Now and forever. Will you marry me?"

"Yes." Jill reaches up, pulls Bill closer to her, and kisses him again. She is conscious of him pulling her tighter and then easing the pressure as his exploration drops below her waistline. When she figures Bill can't wait any longer, she suggests they use the bed. They make love and then fall asleep.

The next morning, instead of going for breakfast, they repeat last night's joy.

On the way to pick up Josey to bring her to the eleven o'clock church service, they agree not to announce their intention to get married until supper at Kathy's. When they meet Josey, they find her in a chipper mood. At first, they suspect she already knows their secret. After the worship service, they discover the reason for Josey's cheerful spirit. Through the church grapevine, Josey leaked the news that she has found her long-lost granddaughter. Church members flock to meet Jill and congratulate Josey on receiving an answer to her prayer. Reverend Andrews, Josey's minister, upon meeting Jill, says he's met Reverend Swanson, Jill's minister. He sends his greetings.

For Jill, the afternoon passes quickly. Josey treats them to lunch at the hotel. After Bill drops her off at McKenzie Manor for her afternoon nap, Jill phones home to announce the news. To her disappointment, her children aren't home. Jill guesses they are visiting Thomas and Rebecca or Daniel. She tries to reach Julie. She fails again. At Bill's suggestion, they take an afternoon nap together, but not before they set the alarm to give Jill time to dress for dinner.

WEDDING PLANS

Kathy's excited announcement, "My sister's coming for dinner," trumps her children's plans. Together with Larry, they eagerly anticipate hearing about Jill's family.

Before dinner is served, Jill coasts through the stories arising from her family album and their many questions. She searches in vain for an opportunity to announce a major change in her life. As everybody sits down at the dinner table, Larry prepares to say grace.

Now, Jill thinks.

A quick elbow nudge and a nod spurs Bill into action.

"Larry, I have something I would like us to thank the Lord for." Bill glances at Jill to confirm that he read her intentions correctly.

"Name it."

"Jill has agreed to marry me."

Shouts of congratulations pour out from around the table. Kathy asks if a date has been set. Out of the corner of her eye, Jill catches Josey flashing an I-told-you-so wink at Bill.

"Not yet," answers Jill. "I'm still recovering from Bill's proposal. I imagine in a week or two we'll figure it out."

"And you'll send us invitations?" asks Kathy.

"Count on it," says Jill.

The conversation alternates between Kathy's dinner and different wedding experiences. Jill's wish for a small family ceremony is lost in the excitement of wedding celebration possibilities. After the meal, Larry, Jack, and Bill escape to the back yard to "work off a few calories." On the way out, Larry grabs three baseball gloves. Josey remains at the kitchen table, watching her granddaughters clear the table and load the dishwasher.

Together, they clean and dry the saucepans used for the meal. It's during this latter task that Kathy glances back to check on her grandmother.

"Uh-oh. I've seen that face before," announces Kathy as she catches Josey deep in thought.

Quickly recovering, Josey says, "Never you mind."

Jill looks at her grandmother and sees nothing different. "What did you see?"

"She's scheming," declares Kathy.

"Am not."

"And she hasn't finished working things out yet. Otherwise, we'd being hearing about it already," says Kathy as she dries her hands and moves to the table. "Okay, out with it, Josey."

"You're kidding," says Jill, following her sister to the table.

Kathy signals Jill to sit. Jill does. "The best time to share in the making of a plan is before Josey has figured everything out." Kathy looks at her grandmother, suspecting wedding plans have been forming. She pushes her advantage. "I've caught you. Now out with it."

"Okay. Okay." Josey's hands go up as if she's being robbed. When her hands rest on the table, she looks at Jill. "Would you like to make two people very happy?" Then she adds, "Bill and me?"

"Here it comes. Here it comes." Kathy's excitement is bubbling over.

"Yes," answers Jill cautiously as she studies her grandmother.

"Remember Bill saying he wants to go to Canada's honeymoon capital?"

"But we're not—" Josey vigorously shakes her head.

"If you extend your holiday and marry him here, he'll have his wish. And if you let me plan your wedding, I'll have a treat I never thought possible."

"Wonderful idea!" Kathy's is so excited she grabs her sister and says, "Jill, say you'll do it. Say you'll do it."

"I can't." Jill looks around for Bill's assistance, but he's not there.

"Why not?" Kathy beats her grandmother.

"Well, my plane ticket—"

"Cancel it. I'll buy you, you and Bill, new tickets." Josey's response sounds like that was one of the details she already worked out.

"The hotel—"

Again, Josey cuts in, assuring Jill she can handle the problem.

"And I'm supposed to be back at work on Wednesday."

"You mean if you tell your boss you're extending your vacation to get married, he'll fire you?" Kathy's objection forces Jill to recognize her sister is probably right.

"No, but it's such short notice. He'll—"

Kathy cuts in. "If he's any kind of a boss worth working for, he'll understand."

Josey reaches out for Jill's hand. In a pleading tone, she says, "Jill, I've been able to do so little for you all my life. Let me do this one really special thing. Believe me. You will love it."

Jill voices her last hurdle. "I have to check with Bill first. He volunteers at the Wellness Center, and he may feel he has to be back soon."

"Well done! She's speaking like a married woman already. Go talk to him."

Jill looks at her grandmother, surprised by the unexpected support. What really stirs Jill is the tone of pride in her grandmother's voice.

It's real! She is *proud of me.* Jill doesn't recall ever generating such a reaction from her grandmother.

Like a queen on the throne, Josey dismisses Jill, urging her to talk with Bill.

As Jill steps out of the kitchen, Josey turns to Kathy and asks, "Want to bet Bill will agree to stay?"

Kathy shakes her head. They hurry to window to watch Bill's reaction. As a result of his facial expressions, a cheer erupts. Bill and Jill turn to see wildly applauding hands.

Jill questions Bill's spur-of-the-moment acceptance. "Aren't there some clients you must see at the Wellness Center?"

Bill explains they'll understand when they hear he is getting married. Again, he reassures her that this is wonderful news. Together, they return to the kitchen to find Kathy waiting for them by the door. Josey sits at the table with a pencil in her hand.

"Josey, family only," says Jill, seeing her grandmother scribbling feverishly on a notepad.

Without looking, Josey responds. "Yes. Yes. Family only. And maybe a couple of friends."

Jill takes a breath to correct her grandmother when Bill nudges her.

"Close friends," adds Josey.

Bill leans close and whispers, "Probably the Martonis." He chuckles.

Before Jill can speak, Kathy whispers in her other ear, "Look at her. She's as excited as a puppy with its first bone."

Jill's giggle temporarily erases her objection. Periodically during the evening, Jill witnesses Josey jotting additional notes or whispering to Kathy. She guesses they're all plans for her wedding. At one point, Jill mentions that her children will miss her wedding in hopes that Josey would change her mind about holding the wedding in Oshawa. Josey's not-to-worry response does little to ease Jill's discomfort.

The following day, Jill intends to follow the commitments she made to Bill—relax and spend time together. She waits until after breakfast to cancel the Tuesday flights home. Then she talks to the hotel clerk about extending their stay. The manager's response surprises her.

"Congratulations! I hear you'll be getting married."

Jill guesses Josey already talked to him. He tells her that later on in the afternoon, she can move up one floor to a room with more space.

When no one in the park is near enough to overhear her conversation with Bill, Jill says, "I can't believe it. Both Sarah and Julie's phones were busy." Jill tried to call them to tell them of the wedding. "I couldn't even leave them a message to call me back."

Bill's calm reassurances settle Jill. They walk hand in hand through the park like they used to Sundays after supper. While Bill remarks about the cool, fresh morning air, the singing birds, he notes Jill's silence. Her body is with him. Her mind is elsewhere. Guessing she has another concern, he asks what else is bothering her.

She looks at Bill and is tempted to deny she has any problems. The narrow focus of his eyes tells her he will worry about her like she is worrying about the wedding plans unless she tells him what is distracting her. She confesses she prefers the wedding to be at home where Julie and her children could be with them. The belief that Amber will be the most disappointed to miss out on her celebration worries Jill. At the same time, she knows any attempt to change plans would disappoint Josey.

"You did tell Josey that you wanted a *family* wedding, didn't you?"

"I did."

"And you believe she is a very capable person?"

"I do, but it's so much for a person to arrange."

"I have a feeling she knows how to get help if she wants it, whether it's from your sister or anyone else she needs. Don't you agree?"

"Yes, but—"

"But you would still like to be in charge just to make sure that things are done right?"

Jill looks at Bill as if he caught her trying to shoplift something from a store. She feels her face turning red, flashing a guilty sign.

"You don't see me being worried about your grandmother's ability to pull this off, do you?"

Jill shakes her head but remains concerned.

"Then I suggest that you take a different, more positive approach." Jill's questioning look tells Bill he caught her curiosity. "You see how excited your grandmother was at Kathy's place once she believed she could arrange our wedding?"

Jill nods.

"Then think of letting her make the arrangements as a thank-you present for giving you the Brampton house."

A small smile crawls onto Jill's face.

"That's better," says Bill. "Now, promise you'll keep that same trusting happy view for the rest of our holiday."

Jill's smile lights up the rest of her face. She promises.

"Good," says Bill. "Because you know I can tell when you aren't happy."

They continue their walk through the park. Jill's attention turns to nature's beauty, testifying to her relaxed nature. For the rest of the day, she honors her promise to Bill. They enjoy their time together. After dinner, she attempts to call Julie and Sarah and again encounters busy signals.

Taking her camera, Jill asks Bill to drive her to her parents' cemetery. They stop first to purchase some flowers. At the graveside, Jill's first shot is of the tombstones resembling the structure of a house. The second picture is a close-up of the inscription. The distance shot Jill takes tells Bill she wants to be able to have some reference points for finding her parents' place in the future.

Wanting to be alone by her parents' graves, Jill says, "I'll meet you in the car soon."

Bill watches her squatting in front of her parents' graveside. "Soon" takes half an hour.

When she sits down with Bill, he asks, "Okay?"

She nods. "I think I'm forgiven now."

Bill gives her a hug and smiles.

They return to the hotel, find a quiet spot on the outside patio, and order a glass of wine. Nothing is said. They just lean into each other and sip their wine.

The following morning, after breakfast, they return to their rooms to brush their teeth. They each find a message waiting for them. "Your presence is requested at Salon One at ten."

At the appointed time, Bill knocks on the salon door. They enter in time to see Josey grab her cane and stand up from the head of an oval table. She is wearing a narrow navy skirt and jacket with a white blouse and a short, multicolored blue scarf, giving her the appearance of a person in charge.

"We done here?" asks the manager.

Josey waves him off and directs the arrivals to take a seat near her. As she sits down, she says, "You would probably like to know more details about your wedding before I show you the room I've booked for your dinner."

Jill nods.

"Amber's a wonderful girl," begins Josey. Following Jill's surprised look, she adds, "I asked Amber to call me. She did, last night. The first thing she asked me to do is say congratulations. It's about time."

Bill laughs, imagining Amber's reaction to hearing they are getting married.

"I had a few dates in mind for your wedding. Of the dates that Reverend Andrews gave me, Thursday, August 18, works the best. Amber said she'd quit work a little early. Before confirming the date with me, Amber talked with Daniel. He said that he and Eve could also make it.

Unfortunately, they decided to leave their children with her parents. I so would have loved to see my great-great-grandchildren."

"Amber will miss at least a week of work," objects Jill. "I'm surprised she can afford it."

Josey grins. "That's probably because she has a possible new source of revenue."

"Like what?" asks Jill.

"Her paintings," explains Josey. "My conversation with her resulted in one sale already. I also told her I know of an art gallery in Oshawa where her paintings can be displayed. And I know of a couple in Toronto. Now that's no guarantee of sales, but if two or three of her works sell, she'll make good money. I convinced her to bring more than a dozen pieces of work when she comes for the wedding."

"And Julie?" asks Jill.

"Talked to her too. She and the children can make it. Scott can't get free."

Seeing Jill's smile, Josey continues, "I knew you would be pleased, but I'm not finished. Julie phoned and asked your friends, Mary and Ed and Pete and Ann to come. And before you say anything, I want you to know that I'll be paying for all their flights."

Anticipating objections, Josey lets four words escape from Jill before she shakes her head. "This is my expense because *I*…" She stresses and repeats the pronoun. "*I* want to see my great-grandchildren. And I simply must see and thank your friends, the ones who took such good care of you when you left here. So I don't want to hear another word about it. Understand?"

Jill nods.

"Good, I'll be giving Julie the name and number of my travel agent. He will take care of everything." In an attempt to sweep away the waves of gratitude from Jill and Bill, Josey stands up with the help of her cane and recommends they talk to Gerald. "He'll show you the room we have booked for the reception. I still have a number of things to arrange."

As they are leaving, Josey calls Jill back. "Close the door," directs Josey when Jill reenters the room. "About Amber's paintings," she begins. "I've talked to Kathy. For Oshawa, for Brampton, and in particular for Toronto, Kathy will take Amber. I'll write a letter of introduction, but Kathy will introduce Amber to the owners of the galleries. Of course, I will have set everything up beforehand. That means Amber will be staying here longer than Sarah and Matthew. But Julie has agreed to have Matthew stay with her, and Sarah said something about a chance to do some horseback riding and staying with Daniel."

Jill nods her understanding and thanks Josey.

"Just one more thing," adds Josey. "I know it's early to ask you this question, but when I told Marvin I sold the property, he became quite anxious. He was wondering when you might be able to tell him if you would be willing to retain his services. I want you to know he does a good job. Of course, if you plan to move out here, he would understand why you wouldn't need him."

There's no hesitation in Jill's response. "Tell him I would be pleased if he would be willing to work for us. Moving out here, as much as I would like to, is not an option. I know how important it is for Bill to be involved at the Wellness Center. I can't take him away from that."

"Bless you, my dear." Josey sets her cane on the table and wraps her arms around Jill. "I was hoping you'd say that. And Marvin will be glad to hear of your decision." When they finish hugging, Josey sends Jill out, saying, "Go. I think Bill has been waiting for you long enough."

After viewing the reception room, which they both judge to be a little larger than necessary, they retire to Bill's room to go online and explore possible tourist sites. Bill recommends going to Ottawa and Montreal before the wedding. After lunch, they tan by the pool and draft a time line to their extended holiday.

The next morning, Jill calls Josey to tell her of the plans for the next four days. A more excited Josey invites Jill over for tea. She has wonderful news. Bill declines Jill's request to come with her.

When Jill enters Josey's suite, she sees Josey's table set—tea, cups, saucers, and a carrot cake. By the teapot are several small notes. Before Jill can announce the plans that she and Bill have made, Josey launches into her news.

"Julie just called me," she begins as she pours tea in Jill's cup. "Everybody's flying down next Thursday."

"Everybody?"

"Your children of course, Sarah, Amber, Matthew, Daniel, and Eve." Josey offers a piece of the carrot cake, which Jill accepts.

"And Julie reached your friends from Edmonton, Mary, Ed, Ann, and Pete. They said they'd love to come. I'm so looking forward to talking to Mary and Ann."

"You're kidding! That's wonderful news!"

"I thought you would like that."

"And Julie?"

"Yes. She's coming with her children."

"You are absolutely wonderful, Josey!"

"But I'm not finished. Thanks to Julie, I was able to reach Bill's pastor, Reverend Williams. He said he'd love to assist your Reverend Swanson in the marriage ceremony."

"You called them both?"

"Yes."

"And they're both coming?"

"Yes. I wasn't sure about Bill's pastor, but I felt sure Reverend Swanson would come. We've had a fair amount of contact."

"But what about Reverend Andrews? We are getting married in his church. Is he okay with it?" Jill blurts out. At the same time, she notes Josey's comment of having known her pastor for some time. *How did Josey know Reverend Swanson?* races through her mind.

"Oh, I checked with him first. He knows your pastor from several conferences. He said he's looking forward to meeting with him again. And that reminds me. They arrive Wednesday morning. Reverends Swanson and Williams asked to meet with you and Bill in the afternoon."

"Both of us?"

"Yes. Then you, Bill, me, and all three pastors will talk."

Jill pauses for a minute while she reviews the plans she and Bill made. "Yes. Bill and I will be back by then."

"Back?"

"Yes. Bill and I have planned on taking a four-day holiday. That's what I was phoning this morning to tell you about. We're leaving tomorrow morning."

"Oh." Josey's surprise comment is accompanied with her sliding far back in her chair.

"Something wrong?"

Josey's pause concerns Jill.

"I take it you haven't heard from Kathy last night."

"No. Why?"

"If I understand Kathy correctly, she wants to take you shopping for a new dress for your wedding. She means for it to be her present for you."

"I haven't heard anything about it. When was she hoping to do this?"

"This Saturday."

Relief sweeps over Jill. Shopping for a new dress for a onetime event is something Jill hopes to avoid.

"We'll still be gone. I can wear what I did when we went out with the Martonis."

Again, Josey falls silent. She rummages around in her notes until she pulls out a business card. "Maybe you could delay your departure by a day." She looks at Jill, still holding the business card. "I took the liberty of phoning a photographer to see if he could take pictures for your wedding. He actually has a booking for next Friday afternoon, but he owes me. He said he'd be willing to rebook his other client if you could confirm you want his services. He asked if he could meet with you. I believe he is available tomorrow morning. Can you make it?"

Questions wrestle in Jill's head, each struggling for a voice. Jill chooses the one that piques her curiosity the most. "He owes you?"

"We both own the business, fifty-fifty, joint ownership. I never ask for a share of the profits. At times, I ask for discounts for friends. When he was starting, that was an excellent way to develop word-of-mouth advertising for him. Since I haven't asked for anything in the last eight years, he has agreed not to charge for your wedding."

Jill's initial reaction to taking pictures is that it is not necessary. Given the photographer's willingness to juggle his schedule for Josey and not to charge, Jill wonders what Bill would say. How would he feel about delaying their departure for a day? Still uncertain if she should accept Josey's offer, she thinks of Kathy's reaction if she declined. It's the reaction from Amber and Julie if there were no pictures that make the difference.

"I think I can convince Bill to stay here another day," she answers. "Who is he?" Jill holds her hand out for the card.

"Good. I'll phone and tell him you'll call and set up a time," says Josey before handing the card to Jill. "I didn't tell him who you were or if you would be interested."

Jill looks at the card, and her mouth drops.

"I know what you're thinking." Josey's response is quick. "You should know that Dave is happily married and has two children."

"Dave!" His name slips out. *Not Mr. Bossard, or Dave Bossard, but Dave, like they're friends or something?*

Jill looks to the table, embarrassed Dave's name slipped out.

"Yes, when you left, he was in the dumps. After almost a year, I convinced him to channel his attention in another area of interest. He chose photography. When he wanted to set up a business, he found he could only raise half the money needed. His savings and some money from his parents showed he was serious. I agreed to supply the balance if he would give discounts to people I sent to him."

Jill listens, not really wanting to hear what her grandmother says. Up to this point, Jill was content that she hadn't heard or seen anything of Dave. Now Josey was pushing her to go see the person she hoped to avoid.

"You *will* call him?" Jill reads the request as a directive. "I think it is something you should do, at least for your own peace of mind."

Jill looks up at her grandmother, wondering what more she knows. *What did Dave tell her?*

Seeing Josey lean forward, like she is preparing to challenge Jill on the wrong answer, Jill nods and then mumbles, "Yes, I'll call him."

"That's my girl." Josey's praise does little to raise Jill's spirits. "Now, I'll phone Kathy. I have to call her at work. We'll see if she can find another time to go shopping with you."

After Josey explains the situation to Kathy, Josey hands the receiver to Jill. Kathy proposes to take Wednesday off, the day after Jill returns from her holiday with Bill. Kathy's eagerness leaves Jill no choice.

Using the excuse that she needs to pick up Bill for lunch, she phones Bill to let him know she's on her way. Jill explains they plan to spend the afternoon shopping for rings. To please Josey, Jill calls the photographer's shop and makes a morning appointment with the secretary. Flashing a smile at her grandmother, Jill leaves. Once she is out of Main Manor, Jill breathes a sigh of relief. *Safe from any more of Josey's surprises.*

Afternoon shopping takes less time than Jill expects. After viewing rings at four different jewelry shops, they both easily agree on the wedding rings. One other ring caught Jill's eye. It most expressed her happiness—a bright-red ruby surrounded by small diamonds.

"Only one detail remains," says Bill. They return to the second-to-last shop for it. "That one. How much is it?" He points to the ruby ring.

Before the clerk can respond, Bill's hand extends a credit card. Out of the corner of his eye, he catches Jill shaking her head. "Don't worry. It's something I can handle."

The clerk promises the ring will be resized in three days.

With the decision made about the rings, Jill's mind slips back to the appointment with the photographer. Bill notes her silence but says nothing until she parks the car at the hotel.

"I think we should take a walk in the park." He doesn't want her disappearing into her room, wrestling with her unresolved issue.

"Should?"

"Should." His confident reply leaves Jill with the impression he knows something is bothering her.

They take the first path that leads into the heart of the park. Bill waits until he sees Jill observing activity around them, a squirrel darting up the tree, a bird landing on a branch to the side, a pansy finding sufficient nourishment and moisture in a crack in the pavement to bloom. "Going to let me in on the secret that's diverting your attention from driving as we came back to the hotel?"

Jill looks at Bill and shakes her head slightly.

Bill smiles, knowing she hates it when he reads her moods, particularly when she feels down.

Jill looks around. It's in the middle of the afternoon. No one is close by. She points to a bench farther up the path. As they near it, Jill opens her purse and takes out Dave's business card. When they sit down, she gives him the card.

"For our wedding?"

Jill nods.

"Great idea!"

"I need to meet with him tomorrow morning. Hope you don't mind."

"No problem. When you're finished, then we can leave for Ottawa. You shouldn't let such little things like that bother you."

A lame thanks from Jill forces Bill to guess there is more that Jill hasn't said. Hoping to encourage her, he asks, "You knew him before?"

Jill nods and then tells him that when she ran away from home, Dave's place was the first place she went to. She also tells about the forced kiss in the pantry.

"You still think he's interested in you, after all this time?"

Remembering that Josey said he was married with two children, she shakes her head. Jill then tells about how she ran away the day before Josey brought Dave to Brampton. She looks for disapproval in Bill's eyes but sees none.

Hesitantly, Bill offers a guess. "Do you think he's still angry with you?" Then another possibility occurs to him. "Or do you still have feelings for him?"

Thinking of Bill's first question, she answers, "I don't know."

"To which question?"

Jill forces herself to remember Bill's earlier questions. "Oh! No. I love you, Bill."

"Do you realize that is the first time you said you love me?"

Jill smiles, hugs Bill, and plants a kiss on his lips. She continues holding on to him, even though she realizes it is unlikely that Dave is still angry with her.

When Jill lets go of Bill, he asks, "So what is bothering you about this Dave?"

The only thing Jill knows is that Dave is or should be angry with her. The moment she asks herself why, she sucks in a deep breath like someone hit her in the stomach.

Three hundred dollars! I stole it! I stole it from Dave! From Dave and Greg! Greg! Oh no.

"Okay. Now I know I've touched a tender tooth. Out with it. You know there should be no secrets between the two of us. Whatever bothers you bothers me. Together, we'll handle the problem." He puts his hand on either shoulder and turns Jill to completely face him.

With tears of embarrassment, she whispers, "I'm a thief."

Bill draws her close to him and holds her until he feels she has quit crying. He eases his hold on her and waits for her to explain her remark. Her prolonged silence prompts him to ask, "What happened?"

As if picking at an old scab, Jill slowly reveals the least-threatening portion of her secret. "I stole three hundred dollars from Dave and his brother, Greg."

Jill waits for a reaction, as if she's waiting to see some blood pour out from the edge of an opened scab. Hearing no hint of judgment, she continues, "They deserved it. It was a punishment."

The moment the condemnation tumbles from her lips, Jill questions what she said. *Did Dave deserve to lose the money?* The answer slaps her into realizing it was Greg's money she stole. It was Greg whose vengeance she needs to fear, not Dave's.

Jill strains to recall if she missed a response from Bill. She remembers no sound coming from him. Worrying over how Bill is receiving this dark side of her, Jill pulls back and looks up at his attentive eyes. She's uncertain if the concern she sees is about what she has done or how she feels about it.

Like one seeing the hard crust of a scab partially free from the skin and begging to be pulled free, Jill exposes her past sin even more. "While Dave was kissing me, Greg stuck his hands in my pants. I was stupid. I knew they were drinking. I shouldn't have been in such a private, secluded place so they could do what they wanted. It was my fault."

"Absolutely not. Don't blame yourself for others' self-centeredness. Their lack of respect for you is their mistake, not yours." Bill's instant response wipes a part of Jill's guilt away.

"I was wrong. I shouldn't have stolen the money. Mom always said two wrongs don't make a right." Jill recalls her mother's often-repeated admonition when Jill wanted to get even with her father for some of the things he said or did when he came home drunk.

"Look. If you don't want this Dave guy to be our photographer, we'll just tell Josey that. I'll support you."

Jill considers Bill's offer. She knows she'd have to explain her refusal to Josey, an explanation that would portray her as lacking in courage to face up to her past, to face up to her mistakes. Such a decision would reveal a trait that would disappoint her grandmother. Jill suspects her grandmother is sending her to see Dave for a reason, a reason that probably is meant to strengthen her.

Recalling Josey's plea to hear Dave on that Monday long weekend, Jill asks, "Do you think Dave can forgive me for running out on him when he wanted to apologize for his pantry mistake?"

Bill takes a breath to respond, but Jill interrupts.

"And for me making myself into a vengeful person, like his brother? And becoming a thief? I was so wrong. Bill, there's so much I did that was—"

Bill's finger rests on her lips, stopping the painful bleeding.

"In the light of the circumstances, your actions are completely understandable."

"But do you think he'll still be angry? Do you think he can forgive me?"

"I do."

"But—"

"Jill, remember the years of anger that Daniel built up toward you?"

Jill recalls Bill's instructions to pray to God and ask for God's and Daniel's forgiveness and God's help. She recalls her apology to Daniel and the healing that followed.

"Would you lead in a prayer?"

Bill nods, and they both bow their heads. "Dear God," begins Bill.

Jill realizes Bill refrained from starting with "Dear Father." While she is grateful for Bill's sensitivity, she also knows that the term, *Father*, no longer burns like it did before. Jill follows Bill's words, listening to his reference to God's compassion, his request for Dave's understanding and forgiveness, and for God's forgiveness and strength for Jill. He concludes that this trial is only one more sign for Jill to see how God stands with her in times of need.

"I like to hear you pray," says Jill. "You seem to know so much more about what I need." She knows her prayer would have been a simple: "Please, dear Lord, help me get through this terrible time."

Bill smiles and plants a kiss on her lips. At that very moment, Jill knows she needs to do something.

"I have to go to the bank," says Jill with conviction. "Today."

"The bank?"

"Yes. I have to withdraw some money."

"For the photography?"

"No. I owe Greg three hundred dollars. Dave can give it to him."

"I'm not sure that's necessary."

"Maybe not. But it tells me I'm doing what I can to right a wrong. I've got to try, Bill. For my own peace of mind."

Bill's eyebrows rise. "Whatever you say."

Jill stands and almost pulls Bill to his feet. In seconds, she is leading the way down that path to the hotel and their vehicle. Bill smiles, seeing the energy and confidence that is part of the woman he loves.

"So when we have finished at the photography studio, we can take off for Ottawa?"

"You bet." Excitement characterizes Jill's response.

"Take off like a couple of thieves escaping after we robbed a bank," says Bill, laughing.

Jill turns, squinting at Bill's remark. In a moment, she laughs, not because of his dubious joke, but because he thinks he's so funny, like some kid. It comforts Jill to see that Bill feels free to risk a questionable remark, knowing that she won't be offended.

FACING DAVE

FIVE MINUTES BEFORE HER appointment, Bill pulls up to Bossard's Photography Studio. "Would you like me to come in with you?"

"Thank you for asking, but no. This is something I have to do on my own." She steps out of the car, blows him a kiss, and confidently walks to the shop door.

Before entering, she pauses, looking at the window display—pictures of weddings, baptisms, and older couples celebrating an anniversary. Pictures captured in ovals, in fogs, in black and whites, and group displays all demonstrate a creative flair that Jill never realized was part of Dave's talents. She wonders if that was the reason why Josey invested with Dave or if it was out of sympathy because Jill unceremoniously ran out on him.

Jill enters the studio and is greeted by an attractive thirtyish woman with short, clipped blonde hair.

"Jill Kreshky to see Mr. Bossard. I've a ten thirty appointment."

The receptionist picks up the phone.

"Dave will be with you in a few moments."

Jill scans the walls of the waiting room. One wall features portraits while another is filled with scenes from all four seasons. Photos of winter poke into spring and spring into summer like trickling water not being confined to any space. As summer scenes claim their space, Dave's voice cuts Jill's admiration of his work.

"Jill Rezley, I mean Kreshky! Am I so happy to see you!" His voice carries from his office door. The joy in his voice causes the receptionist to look at her boss in surprise. By the time Jill stands up, Dave is halfway across the waiting room, his hand outstretched. Jill extends her hand. She feels his energy.

"Come into my office. I have to tell you when I heard the name Jill, I dared to hope it was you. I haven't run across any other Jills. But your surname puzzled me. I was hoping you were the person that Josey said would be calling, that Kreshky was your married name, but then again, Josey talked about wedding pictures, so you can see why I was so confused."

The office door closes as Dave directs Jill to a seat in front of his desk. He grabs the chair from the side his desk and pulls it in front of Jill. "So how have you been?"

"I've had some ups and downs, but since I'm getting married—"

"You came here." Dave raises his hand to signify a high in Jill's life.

"And how are you?" asks Jill.

"Good business. Good wife. Good kids. Good life," fires Dave with a smile and energy Jill can't remember ever seeing in Dave. "Hey! I have to say, I'm so glad to see you. You're looking good."

"I have to tell you, your reaction is unexpected. After I left you, without giving you—"

"Forget that," interrupts Dave. "I figured the jolt I gave must have upset you more than I realized. I was way out of line. I know I was drinking that night, but that was no excuse. I only hope that you can forgive me."

"Forgive you! I came hoping you might forgive me. I mean not only did I prevent giving you a chance to explain yourself on that day that Josey brought you to Brampton, but also I stole money from you, from you and Greg."

"Forgotten and forgiven a long time ago."

As Jill opens her purse, she says, "Still, I would like to return what I took. It didn't belong to me. I imagine it caused some trouble."

"Oh, Greg was so pissed off. It was his money."

"Then you can give it back to him for me?" Jill extends her hand with the money.

"No need. The following day, I took the money from my account to shut him up. It didn't, but it did drain the steam out of his bitching."

"I'm so sorry for the trouble I caused you."

"Don't be. He was a real—" Dave stops searching for a better word than what he almost spilled—*asshole*. "Well, you know what I mean."

Jill nods, her hand still extended with the money.

"Anyway, he's no longer a bother. He died in a motorcycle accident a year last spring. He was drinking."

"Oh, I'm so sorry," says Jill, "for you, I mean."

"Not to worry. He was a source of tension for my parents and me. We now have peace. Hopefully he does too."

Setting the money on Bill's knees, Jill says, "I would like to return the money you paid for me."

"No need." Dave quickly grabs the money as it starts to slide off his knee.

"I appreciate you saying that, but I still would like you to take it. Take it for me. It helps me feel like I've made some amends for my past."

"If it makes you happy, it's the least I could do. I want you to know, these pictures for your wedding, I'd have done them for you for free, a wedding present so to speak. But Josey's already said they are on her. I only hope you'll let me include some experimental creative approaches. If you like them, then that's my present to you; if not, I'll owe you."

"I've seen some of your work when I came in. I'm sure Bill and I will be fascinated by them."

"Bill! I take it he's the lucky man?"

"He is."

"Then I look forward to impressing both of you."

They work on some of the details for Jill's big day and set a time to finalize the remaining arrangements. Jill leaves Dave's shop with a sense of freedom she cannot ever remember. As she joins Bill in the car, she says, "I'm ready, my husband-to-be! Let's start our prehoneymoon adventure."

"Prehoneymoon. I like that."

PREHONEYMOON ADVENTURE

BILL'S FRIDAY MUST-SEE IS Parliament Hill. For Jill, the National Gallery of Canada is her highlight. It captures most of their day. The next day, they begin with Notre Dame Basilica, but they find it hard to break away from the charms of Gatineau Park. While their tentative schedule calls for a morning departure to Montreal, they first take in the beauty of Rideau Canal, imagining what it must be like skating there in the winter.

One key recommendation of Bill's Montreal research was to dine out in Montreal. Sunday and Monday evenings, they enjoy French cuisine. While still in Oshawa, Bill booked them to see some film festivals. The freewheeling spirit that marked their holiday adventure tempts them to stay one more day in Montreal, but Jill knows she must honor her dress-shopping time with Kathy. If Kathy hadn't booked time off work, Jill would have called and tried to postpone the shopping for one more day. When they return to Oshawa, they face a whirl of activity for their family-and-only-close-friends wedding.

Kathy usurps Jill's reluctance for shopping the moment she arrives early at Jill's door. "You get my message?" she says as soon as Jill opens her door.

Jill nods. Her answering machine said the meeting with the pastors was postponed to the evening. Kathy informed Jill that she'd be over early. *Be ready to shop.* Taking her sister at her word, Jill convinces Bill to get up early for breakfast.

"Okay. Let's go have fun." Kathy opens the door to the hall. "We have a dozen places to hit. We'll find the perfect dress for you." With an arm around her sister's waist, Kathy ushers Jill to her car.

"I don't even have an idea of what I am looking for," objects Jill.

"Easy. What makes you feel happy. What else should a dress do for you on your wedding day?"

"And if I don't know what that is?"

"You will when you have it on. Take my word for it. I'm going to make this the best wedding present you'll have."

It takes visiting three dress shops before Kathy's hunting excitement infects Jill and another five stops before Jill proclaims, "It's me!"

Jill's choice is a V-neck multicolored floral print with a white collar and a wide white leather belt. The light material sways with her every movement.

Not completely convinced Kathy asks why this one is the right one.

Jill twists left and right. "Look at the life in it! It's me!" Jill pictures herself with unlimited energy, able to tackle anything. "Look at the colors." For Jill, flowers in full bloom suggest the peak of life. The pattern expresses how she feels about marrying Bill. Pointing to her white belt, she adds, "If it isn't for the arresting white to calm one's vision, you could be swept away in the power of swirling colors." Jill doesn't tell Kathy that the calm of the white belt suggests finding perspective, finding an anchor. It's what she sees in Bill. Jill steps forward and back, to the left and the right, and twirls around again like she's on a dance floor celebrating. "See. Overflowing energy, surplus energy. That's me today, now."

Laughing, Kathy says, "Okay, okay. You have convinced me." She signals for the clerk.

Jill steps into the change room happy. She found what she thought was impossible to find.

Kathy joins her grandmother, Bill, and Jill for supper at the hotel. After their meal, Kathy drives to Markham. Bill, Jill, and Josey meet with the ministers at the church. They are welcomed by Reverend Andrews. He congratulates Jill and Bill on their decision to get married and introduces Josey to the two visiting ministers. Before they begin to deal with the logistics of the event, Pastor Swanson asks to briefly meet with Jill in private. He wonders if Jill's decision for marriage is in any way a reaction to her recent divorce and not motivated by love. Pastor Williams echoes the same concern. Since he spent much time counseling Bill about the loss of his wife, he seeks to determine Bill's true motivation for getting married.

When Reverend Andrews receives a nod of approval from each of his guest ministers, he gathers the group around the meeting table and reviews the steps to be followed during the ceremony. When he asks if there is a particular passage that either of them would like to form the basis of the day's message Jill requests 1 Corinthians 13:4–7, the one on her parents' tombstone.

"It will be like my mother is speaking to me," explains Jill.

"In that case, I volunteer to deliver the message," says Walter Swanson. "Knowing Jill and the passage, I think I know what Mrs. Rezley would have wanted to say." Reverend Williams agrees to lead the rest of the ceremony.

"Are you planning to ask Ed Preszchuk to give you away?" asks Reverend Swanson as he smooths his thin gray hair. He remembers Ed gave Jill away at her first marriage.

"I hadn't given it a thought."

"Jill." Josey places her hand on her granddaughter's shoulder. "I know it's the father's role to give the bride away, but since he isn't here and I'm family ..." She pauses. "It would mean so much to me if I could give you away." Seeing surprise on Bill and Jill's face, she continues, "It would be like I'm giving my wholehearted blessing to your marriage, something I didn't really do for Frank and Alice. I would like to think that would really please your mother."

Josey's pleading expression secures Bill and Jill's permission.

"Oh, bless you two!" Josey struggles to her feet and hugs each of them.

When the question of the maid of honor comes up, Jill informs them that Kathy already claimed that role. Then she looks at Bill. "And for best man, I thought maybe Matthew would be willing?" Jill seeks and receives Bill's approval.

Reverend Andrews confirms tomorrow's morning rehearsal time. That fits Jill's plans perfectly as she is expecting her Alberta guests to arrive by noon. In yesterday's phone call to Julie, Jill learned that Julie has rented a large van to drive Jill's children, her children, Pete, Mary, Ann, and Ed to Oshawa. In anticipating the next afternoon, Josey reminds Jill that she would like to spend some time with Mary and Ed and Ann and Pete. Jill can't help comparing her grandmother to Mary. They both like to know as much as they can about their friends and family.

Josey's announcement that she and Jill will be at the hairdresser's midmorning Friday sparks a surprise response.

"No." Jill's response is firm.

"But the appointments are already made." Josey's rebuttal fails.

"Then cancel mine. My hair will be done up as Mom did it for me."

"Except that your hair will be tucked behind your ears," adds Bill.

"Kathy's already promised to come early to do my hair. She knows exactly how Mom did it."

Josey is momentarily speechless.

Hoping to strengthen Jill's position, Bill adds, "I love Jill just the way she is. She doesn't have to do anything extra special to please me. I think that is a beautiful statement to make to our family and friends who will be there. I'll bet it is something they will applaud."

"Okay. I guess I will go myself," says Josey, limiting the sadness in her voice.

"Maybe Julie will take my appointment," adds Jill, hoping to erase Josey's frown. She succeeds.

"Anything else?" asks Josey's minister.

A moment of silence passes. Josey hesitantly raises her hand. Her uncharacteristic response focuses everyone's attention on her.

"Yes?" inquires Reverend Andrews.

"Just one more thing." She looks at Bill and Jill. "I know I haven't talked to you about this, but while you were gone, I had the strangest dream. I think we were coming to rehearsal, but it could also have been the wedding itself. Anyway, as we finished and you were leaving the church, bells rang. They rang and rang. I felt like they were angels rejoicing over your commitments to each other."

Josey turns to her minister. "Now, I know our church has a policy that restricts the ringing of bells for only special occasions, like Easter and Christmas, for the sake of the neighbors. But I would like to submit that this is a special time. How often can anyone claim to have found a long-lost granddaughter and then witness her marriage? I would venture to say if you ask anyone in our church, they would all say this qualifies for a special occasion to announce to the community at large. If anyone calls to complain, I would be more than willing to explain my request and if need be ask for forgiveness."

"Forgiveness instead of permission, hey?" says Reverend Andrews.

"Oh please. The wedding ceremony is in the afternoon, so we won't likely be waking anybody up." Josey reaches out for Reverend Andrews arm.

Reverend Andrews looks to Jill and Bill. When he sees Jill's vigorous approval, he acknowledges the circumstances are unusual. He notes he will be the one who has to take full responsibility for the decision, and he agrees.

Out in the parking lot, Jill notices Josey is shaking more than usual. "You tired?" she asks, pointing to her grandmother's hands.

"Excited," says Josey.

Ordinarily, Josey takes pleasure in sitting back and watching everything she's planned come together. Her success rate means she has no reason to be nervous, but her granddaughter's wedding is an exception.

Sensing more of an explanation is required, Josey adds, "This is like being on a bus tour. You stop for lunch at a café, briefly meet the owners, and then you're on your way. It's all so fast." She looks at Jill to see if she understands. "I want to make a good impression on your children. We'll have had so little time together."

"I wouldn't worry about that if I were you," says Pastor Andrews as he pats her on her shoulder. They walk slowly to Kathy's car. She's talking on her cell, responding to a call from the office.

The pastor continues, "I'm sure everything you set up will work perfectly. This afternoon, Jill's family and friends will be here. You've arranged it so the hotel will accommodate them all. Your photographer friend, Mr. Bossard, seems eager and ready. You're a master organizer. Everything will work out. And if I heard Kathy correctly, you're flying everyone down here at your expense ..." He pauses until he sees Josey's confirmation nod. "All that testifies to your kindness, your generosity. How can anyone not be impressed?"

Josey reveals her real source of anxiety. "I guess what really bothers me is that I'll have so little time to get to know them. Sarah and Matthew will only be here for two days, and then they fly back. And the same is true for Jill's friends. At least Amber will be around a little longer."

"Then invite them back for a longer visit next year." Josey's minister smiles as he observes the usually unflappable Josey in turmoil. *This saint is human after all*, he thinks. He knows under normal circumstances, she would be giving the same advice that he just gave her.

Kathy is still talking on her cell when Pastor Andrews opens the car door for Josey. As she settles herself, he says, "Don't worry, Josey. Everything will work out as it should. When this is all over, you'll count this as one of the best times of your life."

After a light lunch at the hotel, Josey excuses herself. Before going to Kathy's hotel suite for a catnap, she instructs Kathy to wake her as soon as company arrives. After securing Kathy's nod, Josey's fixes her eyes on Jill and Bill and mines a similar commitment. Josey reluctantly leaves.

Not fair, Josey mutters as Kathy gently shakes her shoulder.

"Company's here." The familiar cheerful voice counters Josey's desire not to get up.

"Just fell asleep," Josey feels like saying.

Kathy pulls the drapes, and the afternoon sunlight floods the room. Josey struggles to sit on the edge of the bed. Once she recognizes the room, she grabs her cane and shuffles to the bathroom where she runs a comb through her hair. A glance at her watch tells her she slept for more than an hour.

"How long ago did they come?" Josey is suspicious Kathy let her sleep too long.

"Not that long ago. They've registered and are probably unpacking now." Kathy finishes straightening out the bedcovers.

"Ready?"

Together, they make their way to the pool area where Jill, Bill, and Matthew await. Josey's great-grandson enjoys a twenty-minute exclusive audience, until his sisters arrive. His most exciting news is that Bill asked him to be his best man.

"Here they come," announces Bill as he points to two girls in short shorts and sleeveless tops covering their bathing suits.

Jill introduces her daughters. Josey stands up for a hug from them.

"What's this?" asks Jill in surprise as she points to a yellow rose tattoo on Amber's right arm.

"And I have a horse's head on the other one," announces Amber as she turns for Jill and Bill to admire it.

"Me too!" Sarah shows off her tattoos to Josey.

Sensing disapproval coming from Jill, Josey examines the artwork carefully. Her praise about the quality succeeds in muzzling Jill's objection and earning the girls' admiration.

Reading his mother correctly, Matthew nudges Bill. He whispers in Bill's ear after inclining his head toward his sisters, "Dodged a bullet."

Bill smiles and nods.

Sarah and Amber hold Josey's attention until Julie arrives with John-Ryan and Jeff-Roger. Amber introduces them. Splashing water attracts the attention of John-Ryan and Jeff-Roger. Other boys are descending down the water slide. "Go," says Julie. Her children race off. The appearance of a beach ball fails to pull Sarah and Amber into the pool. Mary and Ed and Pete and Ann arrive. When Josey's attention switches, the girls dive into the pool. Soon a volleyball game is underway.

Josey trades retirement stories with her new arrivals. A gesture from Josey brings Carla, a hotel employee, to her side. In response to Carla's whisper, Josey nods and dismisses the hotel employee like she's her personal servant. Ten minutes later, Carla carries a shiny silver tray with several ornate cups. A silver teapot sits in the middle. Another employee presents a tray of assorted desserts.

After they are served, Josey looks at Mary and Ann. "I look at you two like a good book, a best seller. I can hardly wait to open your cover and learn the stories of Jill, the Camrose country girl."

Mary glances at Jill and winks, assuring her she'll only relate the best stories as if they consulted beforehand. Julie had told Mary and Ann to expect Josey to pry everything she could out of them about Jill. Bill is fascinated by Mary's stories about Ben's interest in Jill and Joseph's fumbling courting efforts. By the time Ann finishes sharing her stories about Jill's church involvement, Josey announces dinner will be served in half an hour. Waving Amber to come from the lounger where she's tanning, Josey invites her to bring her paintings to supper.

Amber's private art show starts after all the supper orders have been taken. One suitcase holds a dozen of Amber's paintings. She describes various techniques she used in her work and identifies the locations: the banks of the North Saskatchewan River, their former farm, Daniel's place, Edmonton winter roads, and skating at Hawrelak Park.

Josey announces she is purchasing the painting with a scene showing an undernourished rose behind shiny black iron bars. The rose, bearing tiny blossoms and equally small green leaves, is nestled among three granite boulders. Bordering each side of the rose a little distance away are two thick maple trunks that cast a shadow that reaches across the lawn. In the distance, sun-spotlighted, is a jet-black paved driveway that stretches to a grand old house. Like people lining a parade route is a row of bushy roses.

Turning to the manager, who has come to confirm that all was as she wished, Josey asks, "So which work do you think would go well in the lobby over the registration desk?"

The manager bends down to ask Josey for a clarification. She tells him she's donating his choice to the hotel. He feels relieved he isn't incurring an unapproved expense.

He considers two paintings. One is a work looking over the North Saskatchewan River in the fall. A high bank reveals various sedimentary layers screened behind scattered poplars. After consulting with Josey, he chooses the second, a scene from Daniel's yard. In the midst of skeleton birch trees is an apple tree. Many green leaves still tenaciously cling to the branches. Near the top, out of everyone's reach, hangs a single red apple, surveying the yard. Josey identifies with it. She pictures it as a queen mother confidently surveying her realm.

"Congratulations, Amber," Josey announces cheerfully. "This evening, you made two sales. I predict many more in the future."

MARRIED

"I NOW PRONOUNCE YOU HUSBAND and wife." Reverend Williams's voice still rings in Jill's ears, as does the applause from family and friends clustered in three pews behind the newly married couple. The three pastors, standing before Mr. and Mrs. Wynchuk, lead the gathering in the singing of "When Peace Like a River," the song chosen by Jill's pastor, Reverend Swanson. Singing softly, Jill enjoys hearing Bill confidently echo the words of those behind them. After completing the first three verses and the refrain, Pastors Andrews and Williams drift to the pew next to Kathy and Larry and their two children. Josey's friend and pianist, Norma, sits beside her.

Jill's pastor begins by reading the first seven verses of 1 Corinthians. "Thank God those words inspired Jill's mother. I hear it formed the basis for her marriage. I pray that they are being inscribed on the hearts of Bill and Jill. For you know …" He pauses and looks directly at the husband and wife before him. "You have nothing if you don't have love. And I am overjoyed to announce that you two are not bankrupt. You each have a sincere love for each other. But you should also know that you have the undying love of God, the Father. Who else do you think would have brought the two of you together when you most needed each other?"

Reverend Swanson looks at them for another confirmation. The Wynchuks nod in unison.

"So that you don't ever lose this wonderful quality of love that cements your relationship, let us examine, remember, and protect it."

Jill follows the words of her pastor until he focuses on "keeps no record of wrongs." Jill's mind races to her mother and how she always seemed to be able to defend her father as if he'd done no wrongs. Jill recalls her mother never accusing her father of anything. She never tallied the times he said or did things that hurt her.

She was so loving! Jill promises to be more like her.

Reverend Swanson's reference to "always protects" intrudes on Jill's commitment. Memories of Jill noting the number of times that Joseph spent time with Daniel rise. The presumption that he desired to steal him away from her embarrasses Jill. An inkling of her role as stressor in her past marriage scratches Jill's conscience.

A flash of light from behind and above her pastor catches Jill's attention. Dave's quick, apologetic smile and shrug of his shoulder precedes his quiet disappearance. A movement floating to her side assures her Dave is sparing no energy to capture special moments.

He began shortly after Kathy styled Jill's hair. While Jill's hair camouflaged most of her face, Dave called for a time of crazy fun poses. He convinced Jill to look down at the floor. Then, while standing on a chair, he had her turn his eyes up to him.

"Dave!"

Jill's exclamation marked her reactions to Dave's numerous playful efforts to trigger joyful images. Caught in his playful spirit, she gave him a pout face when he called for it. A more lifelike expression emerged when he claimed Jill's mother said she couldn't go outside. Minutes before Julie arrived to drive Jill and Kathy to the church, he took shots of the two sisters embraced, looking in the mirror, and glancing at their watches. When her first happy face shot failed to impress him, he asked Jill to image Bill's kiss after the announcement that they are husband and wife. Dropping to the carpet for a worm's-eye view of the bride, he caught Jill looking down and laughing at his childlike attempt to pull a reaction. At times, Jill imagined Dave thought his task was to entertain her as well as take her pictures.

Reverend Swanson's words, "And so as Jill's mother's final words so succinctly said," pull Jill to the present. Her pastor concludes his message. Jill glances at her watch. *Short! Like he said it would be!*

As the two Alberta pastors sing the closing hymn, "Lord, Today Bless This New Marriage," Julie's two boys and Reverend Andrews slip away with only Josey noticing. Dave, who, like a fly that couldn't sit in any one spot for long, scurries halfway down the aisle to take pictures of the married couple leaving the church. After several shots, he darts out the door and down the steps where he wheels around. The moment the doors open, Dave waves a signal to the bell tower. John-Ryan and Jeff-Roger start ringing the church bells. Having forgotten the final touch, Bill and Jill look up in amazement. Reverend Andrews waves. Dave captures the Wynchuks' surprise, the pastor's waving, and the guests offering their congratulations.

According to plan, Daniel taps Bill on the shoulder and with Eve, scampers down to their car, the wedding car, decorated this morning by Amber and Sarah. Dave records the departure, including shots of Daniel's car leaving with the *Just Married* sign on the back and Jill looking out the rearview window. The car rolls past the church's property line. The bells cease to ring. As if an answer to an unasked question, Jill grasps the meaning of the bells she has so often heard—angels announcing a blessing bestowed on God's child.

When the bells stop ringing, Josey turns to Norma. "Your husband did it!"

"He told the board, the short ringing of bells is no different than wedding cars blowing their horns." Norma is proud her husband listened to her when she said, "Don't ask the board. Tell them."

Pointing to the disappearing wedding car, Josey says, "A glimpse of heaven for them."

Norma pokes Josey. "For you too."

Josey laughs.

"He's wonderful!" Jill points to Dave as she sits on a park bench with her grandmother. To give the wedding couple a break, Dave focuses on other members of the family. Jill's particularly pleased that Dave suggested photos in the park across from her hotel. Using the water fountain as a backdrop is a plus.

"I gave him a list," says Josey. "I haven't seen him consult it once."

"He certainly seems happy."

"He is now."

"Now?" Jill looks at her grandmother.

Josey studies her granddaughter, trying to decide if she should explain.

"Josey?" Jill's coaxing encourages Josey to reveal her secret.

"Just between the two of us?" Josey's voice drops.

Jill nods and leans closer.

"That long weekend in Brampton, the weekend you left, I told Dave that you might not be there. He refused to believe me. He came anyway and talked to Karen and, and that other lady."

"Linda," offers Jill.

"Yes. I think that's who it was. Anyway, Dave was devastated. Moped around for two years. Can you imagine?"

Jill recalls how she felt when Joseph left her. She nods in answer to Josey's question.

"He kept dropping over for a visit. Hoping, I guess, that I might hear a word from you. When his visits became less frequent, I became worried." Josey feels uncomfortable with the revelation.

Jill touches her grandmother's hand; her eyes plead for her to continue.

"I admired his persistence. I felt as long as he had hope that I would hear from you, then I too, should keep my hopes up. I suspected his persistence was becoming an embarrassment to him, so I encouraged him to start a photography business. He'd been doing several little jobs already, sort of like part-time work. That really perked him up. When we met, he could pretend it was for business. I could tell he still missed you. It took three more years before he started going out with Lori. A year later, they married. Another half year and then she was pregnant. By then, he was more like you see him now."

The words *hopes, perseveres* on Alice Rezley's tombstone come back to Jill. *He did love me.*

"Time heals all wounds." Josey's confident statement offers comfort.

Jill's thoughts switch to Joseph. *He loved me too.* Regret clouds her face.

"Jill?" Josey's voice cuts into her granddaughter's reflections.

Jill seizes on Josey's last words—"Time heals all wounds."

"Jill? You all right?"

The worried look on Jill's face is reflected on her grandmother's. Seeing Bill walking quickly toward them, Jill points to Bill and says, "With him around, how can I not be all right?"

As Bill nears, he says, "Dave wants us for more pictures."

Saturday morning comes too fast. Josey booked a private room for a breakfast buffet. The wedding party gathers one more time. Promises to keep in touch lead to exchanging contact information. The afternoon drive to Toronto and the flight to Edmonton prevent stretching the goodbyes. Hugs and tears mark the after-hotel checkout in the lobby. Julie's children climb into the van. While Mary, Ed, Pete, and Ann join them, Matthew and Sarah go back in Daniel's car to catch their afternoon flight. A last set of hugs leads to Bill and Jill driving off to Niagara Falls. Kathy and Amber drop Josey off at McKenzie Manor before they drive to Kathy's home.

Bill prepares Jill for their time in Niagara Falls by describing attractions he wants to see. Early in his drive, he talks about the sights they should be able to see by booking a Double Deck bus tour. She hears of the Rainbow Bridge, Maid of the Mist, and Floral Clock Garden. Punctuated by Jill's occasional agreeing, Bill drones on about wanting to see Clifton Hill, the Falls Incline Railway, and Niagara Botanical Garden and walk through the Queen Victoria Park.

Unknown to Bill, a debate is raging in Jill's head. Should she ask her husband a very delicate question? His answer would mean he would be breaking a promise of secrecy. *Dare I ask him to break his promise? Bill said we shouldn't have any secrets between us.* Jill decides to abandon her request, but guilt reasserts itself. *Would he be hurt if I ask him? I mean, it's not the kind of question a husband would expect from his new bride. Maybe if I explain first why I want the address, it would make a difference.* By the time they arrive at their motel, Jill's dilemma remains unresolved.

"You're early, sir," says the young man at the counter. "But your room is ready."

"Thank you."

"And I have your tickets for the *Oh Canada Eh?* Dinner Theater. Silver seating for tonight, like you asked."

"Dinner theater?" Jill draws closer to the counter and tugs on Bill's sleeve.

"I told you about it on the way down. It's a musical comedy show."

"A must-see," adds the counter clerk. "It's in its sixteenth season and features a five-course meal, a singing Mountie, a hockey player, Anne of Green Gables, and others. You'll love it."

"It highlights Canadian music—maritime folk songs, patriotic ones, rock 'n' roll classics," says Bill. "And I understand the cast also acts as servers too." Bill looks to the clerk for confirmation.

"I've heard some of the servers flirt with their guests." The clerk looks at Bill with a sly smile.

"So that's what attracted you." Jill looks at Bill. Hooking her arm under his, she adds, "I'll have to make sure I keep a close eye on you."

"Thanks again. Trevor, is it?" asks Bill, squinting at the name tag.

"Yes, sir."

Before leaving the counter, Bill asks for directions to Clifton Hill and where to purchase tickets for the Double Deck tour. He's pleased to hear everything is within a fifteen-minute walking distance.

Since they have a couple of hours before dinner, they take Trevor's advice and drive on Niagara Parkway leading to Fort Erie. The attraction here is the luxury homes that line the drive. To savor the scene, they park on the side and join other people walking along the road. Bill notes that while Jill enjoys their walk, she is quieter than usual. Her meditative state continues until they return to their vehicle.

"Sorry I did all the planning for our Niagara holiday?"

"No." Jill's quick, calm answer surprises Bill.

"So what's on your mind?"

Jill looks at him.

"You've been very quiet."

Jill builds her courage. After a few minutes, she says, "You took quite a chance marrying me."

Astonished, Bill looks at her, trying to figure out what prompted that thought. "I don't think so."

"I wasn't a very good wife for Joseph. I can see many times when I acted without caring how it affected him." Jill doesn't look at Bill. She keeps walking at a steady pace.

"You had skeletons haunting you. You've faced them. You've changed." Bill looks at Jill to see if his assurances have any effect.

"Maybe I haven't."

"What do you mean?"

"You remember you said there should be no secrets between the two of us?"

"Yes. I said together we'd handle any problem."

"Then I have to ask you to share a secret that you have, something you haven't told me."

Bill stops. Jill turns and faces him.

"I know you promised Joseph that you would keep his address a secret. I want you to give it to me. You see, I was really hurt when he left me." She pauses, knowing she only revealed half the truth. "Really angry too. I can see that I often acted without considering Joseph's happiness. I hurt him. Maybe made him angry too. I'd like to change that. For his birthday, I'd like to send him a rose to plant. I'd have it delivered from some nursery near his place. He loves roses. I know it won't make up for the hurt I caused, but it will say to me that I'm no longer angry with him. I don't want anger to be a part of who I am. I want to make amends. But, as I said, I'll need his address."

"You know if he sees something is from you he'll probably reject it."

"Yes. But I would send it anonymously. It's not important that he knows that the rose comes from me. Knowing that the plant will put a smile on his face is enough. I owe him that much at least."

"Now that's the girl I always knew was hidden in you, the girl I so much want to be with for the rest of my life." Bill plants a kiss on her lips.

"Then you'll give me his address?"

Bill fishes the cell from his pocket, scrolls through notes, and produces Joseph's address. "Any time you want it."

"Thanks." She kisses Bill. "And if he asks you if it came from me, you can always say you sent it. Together, we'll make his life a tiny bit more enjoyable."

Bill opens the car door for Jill and says, "So we're ready to enjoy tonight's dinner theater?"

"You bet," says Jill. "The dinner and everything that is to follow."

Printed in the United States
By Bookmasters